NEON PROTOCOL

By:

Orry W. von Diez

Printed in the Empire of the United States of America

First Printing 2021

NeonProtocolBook@gmail.com

ISBN: 978-1-7348567-2-9

With a special thanks to my editor (you know who you are).

Chapter Listing

NEON PROTOCOL

Chapter 1

Eleven PM on the dot. The smoke from my cigarette danced above the desk in the rays of neon light, piercing through my window shades. The pitter-patter of rain was the only sound to disturb the silence, aside from my occasional inhaling. The lights were off; who needs 'em, when the city's are always on. It had been a long day, just like every other fucking day. Insomnia? No, I just couldn't sleep; what's the fucking point? I leaned back in my chair. God, I love this chair. The smooth, brown leather was perfectly formed to my frame after years of use. Cushiony, soft, it was just right. I looked forward every day to sitting in this thing. All of my woes were gone in this chair. I felt invincible here, like nothing could derail my train of thought, like nothing could fuck my shit up worse than anything that happened even two minutes before I plopped my ass down in this glorious chair. The arms were just the right height. It reclined just right: just right so that I could lean back, and gaze out at the city that abused me every day. And, I could exhale a fat cloud and think, 'fuck you.'

Just as I reached for my pack of smokes, the phone rang. That annoying sound only means that someone wants something from me, and right now, I couldn't give a shit less. I answered: "Peiler." "Hey, Johnny, you fuckin' willy-wizard, where you at man? I got another case down at the precinct, we need that autism of yours again. Get your chain-smokin' ass down here." God, I hate that guy. 'That guy' was my boss, unfortunately, and my job was never over. Never. "Alright, I'll see you in thirty." With that, I hung up and let out a sigh of exhaustion. I looked over to the corner of the room at my fat cat. "Ain't no rest, huh?" "Meow." Typical response. I grabbed a cig from the pack, lit it, took a long drag, and leaned back in my chair. "Nah, there ain't no rest," I stated while looking out of my 46th floor window. "Ain't never any fuckin' rest."

I got up to grab my jacket, passing my messed up bed with laundry strewn over it. My only real book — some fiction called *Holy Bible,* something about a cosmic war, talking snakes, and magic — was tossed on top of the clothes heap. Probably not the best place for that. I forgot to close the fridge again, who knows how long it was open. Milk probably went bad, not like I drink enough of it anyway. 'Least the liquor won't spoil from neglect, unlike my fucking heart. When did I become so dead inside? Must have been years ago because I can't recall, not that I can recall much anyway. In fact, I'd rather not. Where the fuck are my keys? How do you lose anything in a one room apartment? Two, if you count the bathroom. All I had was a desk, a bed, a fridge, and that amazing chair. I grabbed my coat from the hanger on the back of the front door. "Ofcourse, my keys are in the pocket, and the wallet too." I seem to forget that I always keep my things in my coat; where else am I to put them without forgetting them? A sneering laugh escaped my lips as I slipped my coat on. "Fuck," almost forgot the smokes.

Opening my door, I'm blinded by the fluorescent blue hall lights. What an oppressive place. I threw my black visor shades on. The tromp of my boots echoed against the iron walls. A foul stench filled the air. Only the occasional drip from a leaky pipe interrupted the somber atmosphere of the hall, as I made my way to the elevator shaft. The walls were greenish blue, stained from years of human contact and decay. A film of grime covered everything. *Drip, drip, drip* I hit the button for 'down,' and waited. The sound of mechanical devices straining to do-their-best, emanated from behind the lift doors. What the fuck could possibly necessitate my coming to the station at this hour? Another murder? Maybe they finally caught the guy that was raping androids in District 24B. Wouldn't that be the day. What the fuck is wrong with people?

What I wouldn't give for two minutes alone with that lunatic. *Drip, drip, drip*

The 'ding' of the elevator arriving broke my ruminating long enough for me to look over my right shoulder down the other hall. Approaching me was a tall, busty, slender woman. She was wearing the most atrociously offensive turquoise faux fur halter top with an equally offensive matching miniskirt. Her bright orange, platform stiletto-heeled shoes made her easily two metres tall. She had a bob-cut, neon orange hair, just like those train wreck shoes. "Hey, Johnny, heading out for the night? Want some company?" "Shut off, Tracy, you know I don't dip my pen in electric ink." "Okay, asshole, drop dead, why don't ya?" The elevator doors opened and I went inside. Tracy was standing in the hall glaring at me with those glossy, pitch black eyes. "You know I can't wait to die, sweetheart." "Fuck you, Johnny." "In your non-existent dreams, tin tits," with a shit-eating grin and a half-smoked cigarette hanging from my lips; I flipped her the bird, right as the elevator doors shut.

If there's one thing I can't stand, it's flesh fucking steel. What nut-job stoops so low that he has to get his rocks off with those walking fleshlights? Some sad bastards actually marry those. Shit should be illegal. I inhale a long drag from my cigarette as I lean against the back of the lift. It smelled like vomit, and *lo and behold*, there was the origin of the putrid stench in the corner. What a great place. The fluorescent light flickered as I descended to the ground level.

'*Ding,*' the lift doors opened. "Kill me," I muttered, mustering every ounce of my being to wrench myself from the wall I was leaning on. Hands in my pocket, I walked towards the entrance of the main lobby. Despite the size, there was practically nothing in this lobby. There was a reception desk to my right and a couple of couches to my left, along the wall. A stain covered and chipped mosaic tile pattern bejeweled the floor. Never really caught my interest to study it. *"Have a safe night, Mr. Peiler,"* came a robotic voice from behind the desk. I simply motioned to the 'droid with my hand and kept walking. Stepping into the glass revolving door, I flipped the collar of my jacket up around my ears.

Perpetual daylight accosted me. Not natural by any stretch, simply that there were so many lights that everything was either neon or shadow. Puddles of water gathered everywhere, slicked by oil and filth. A fine grit hung about everything, nothing was clean, nothing was pristine. The concept of *immaculate* was so utterly foreign that not a soul minded their existence in such a dreary hellscape. They all just went about their lives like vermin or insects, oblivious to their conditions like the cattle they were.

The news stand in front of my complex always had something interesting on the Holoviewer™. I should probably have a look before heading to the precinct. "Wu-chin, what's the buzz on the HV today?" "Ohhhh, Mista Peirer, you ah up rate? Hahaha, you must'a be on your way to sorve a crime!" "You know me, Wu-chin, always the vigilant hero." "Da newrs won' say it, but'a rumor has it, some chirdren went missing again in da district, somet'ing bad happening, I know it." Fuck, Curden doesn't give a damn about these missing-children cases and yet he calls me in at midnight for, more than likely, some bullshit. "Hey, let me get a pack of Outer Rims™ and a can of Orbit™, decaff." "You wan' Outer Rim™ mentawr, regurar or unfirtered?" "Wu, we go over this every other day, unfiltered, please, alway-.."A sudden crash interrupted me. I wheeled about on my heel, reaching into my jacket to grab my gun. It was a car crash. Rushing over to the now gone driver-window, "Sir, are you injured?!"

The guy was seemingly unconscious. Just my luck. I yelled back over to the news stand, "Wu-chin, call the medical service!" He quickly began tapping on his holopad. Alright, they should be here in about five minutes. Opening the badly damaged driver door, I managed to secure the pilot in place. I began to assess him for any major trauma or bleeding. Looks like the safety features of his car saved him, but he must have hit the wall of this building pretty hard because he was out cold. "Still breathing," I stated, standing back upright. Leaning against the car, I reached for my smokes. Last one, convenient. Rain fell all around me as I craned my neck back, exhaling into the air. You rarely notice how pretty the city can be from this angle.

Sirens filled my ears as red lights flooded the area. The ambulance hovered overhead, looking for a decent spot to land. Good luck, this place is a wreck. Eventually it landed near the crashed vehicle, and the rear opened, releasing a couple paramedics. "Jumpin' Jack Christ it took you guys long enough," I shouted, still reclining against the car while smoking. "Who are you?" a confused medic retorted. "Peiler, Special Jurisdiction Unit, badge 88, and you're fucking late." "You kiss your mother with that mouth?" "Yours doesn't seem to mind, now do your fucking job, blood mopper," I flashed my badge at the medics, then stood upright, and walked back over to the newsstand to get out of the way. "Wu-chin, you got my shit?" "Yessir, Mista Peirer, here you go." He slid the smokes and drink across the clear glass counter. "Thanks, charge my account." I opened the pack and lit a new cig with the cherry of my last one. Cracking open my Orbit™, I downed it in one chug. Tossing the can into a nearby receptacle, I started down the street toward the precinct. God damn, I hate this city.

Chapter 2

It was usually a twenty minute walk to District 21 where the Precinct was located, so I always had a decent amount of time to contemplate how much everything sucked. I tended to gauge my trips based on how many cigarettes I could smoke before I got from *A* to *B*. It took me two cigs to get from my complex to the Precinct, so I averaged one every ten minutes. My walk was particularly dreary tonight. Everything seemed a little more lifeless than usual. But at least now you could observe the local wildlife of District 20C, AKA: the homeless and other street-urchins, out foraging in the heaps of trash carpetting the streetsides and alleys. 20C was unfortunately where I happened to dwell. It was one of twenty-seven districts in Metropol 20. Luckily, I don't live far from the next district; otherwise, I'd have to drive to work.

The clack of my boots echoed against the towering concrete reminders of my imprisonment. What exactly is freedom in a place like this? Constantly oppressed by the lights, the sounds, the signs; always an advertisement for something:

Everything You Need
For Your Paradise

Who knows what this ad's selling, but I know nothing around here fits the description of a "paradise." Neon ads, selling everything from sex to surgery; you could buy it all – and they reminded you of that fact every moment of your life. There was always some pink silhouette of a shapely woman beckoning me into one of a thousand shifty dope-dens. It wasn't just lights either, no, that would be a waste of money. After all, there were five dimensions, which meant five times the advertising space:

"Buy Po'Flex™ watches; You'll die before it does, or your credit back!"

"Femoid®'s XXX; Best Suck for your Buck!"

"B.J.Nickel's™; Fifty Percent off all Men's underwear when you buy any two dress-shirts!"

Everywhere you went, you were accosted by sales, constant stimuli. It broke the individual down, made you exhausted, and you never seemed to know why you could never get enough sleep. In all honesty, I could use another shirt or two. But, most of these ads are just noise, unpleasant noise. At least the sound of walking is always pleasant.

That pleasant sound of wet concrete gritting beneath my shoes; the echo of it, it commands a presence. Sound can make, or break, any situation. The animals I interact with on a daily basis are easily understood by their most base instincts; and nothing spooks a beast like the right sound. And in that reality, it was getting pretty spooky around here all of a sudden. An eerie silence had crept up on me faster tha- *BANG*

With gun-in-hand, I wheeled about at an instant, only to see the silhouette of a humanoid, darting down an alley to my now-left. I wasn't shot, nor, I decided with a glance, was anyone else on the street. Rushing over to the entrance of the alley, I peered around the corner, careful not to get my block dusted. Forgetting myself momentarily, I had to think of how cool it sounded to run down that empty street. It's like a movie. "Heh, what the fuck are you doing?" escaped my lips, and I snapped out of my fantasy. I didn't see anyone down the alley, it's like he – *but there he was*! Scampering up to the second story walkway of the above level. It was spectacular to witness his agility.

"We'll meet again, you fucking punk!" I yelled after him. Not my finest moment, and definitely not my ideal conclusion to a movie script. Lighting another cigarette, I continued towards the precinct. And, just my luck, it started to rain.

I could never get used to looking at this monolith and thinking, 'Ya, I work here.' It's the only white building in the entire city, as far as I know. How it stays clean is a mystery, though, I'm sure that's what the "missing" budget expenses help fund. Personally, I'd rather get a bigger salary. But, who's complaining, I eat. Albeit, I wouldn't truly consider this processed shit, food, that they feed us. At some point in the past, they had to have had real food that inspired all this fetid garbage they try to pass on to us as edible in the modern era. But, that's neither here nor there, is it. You really have to stop and wonder, if it's even worth getting up in the morning for. The automatic doors opened with a brisk enthusiasm, welcoming me into the spiritual abyss that was GDC Precinct 21™. "Fuck, I can't smoke in here." Flicking my cig into the trash receptacle, I entered the building. A cool air rushed over me, sending chills down my spine. It didn't help that I was soaked to the bone in whatever acid-rain the city felt kind enough to bestow upon my wretched hide.

Everything inside looked to be comprised of some kind of ultra-smooth, sanitized, white plastic. It coated everything. The floors, the walls, the pillars, the desks – everything. Seams between things emanated a piercing, white-yellow light. *The Heaven of Hell* was a fitting nickname. You couldn't see them, but you were being watched by countless little cameras. Not a millimetre of this place went outside of the supervision of those fucking cameras.

We Watch You for Your Safety..

..went the slogan of the Global Defense Corporation®. The "G.D.C.," if you're trying to be a clown. 'Boots Global' stands as the premier public sector Police Force, '*offering nothing less than the best for your Civic Investment...*' or so they said. At least it pays well enough to keep me out of public housing. Who knows, I could even get a promotion. Imagine having a separate kitchen, or an office, or maybe even a living room: the possibilities are endless with another room, it's almost mind-boggling. I honestly wouldn't know what to do with the space, and quite frankly, the whole idea is a little indulgent, and indulgence isn't a luxury I can afford right now or possibly ever, so why dream?

"*Special Jurisdictions Unit 88, Agent, Peiler, Johnathan. What a pleasure to see you tonight. Is there anything I can prepare for you while you are en route to your destination?*" The words closed in around me from every angle. The voice was robotic, soothing, feminine, yet shook the innards like the deepest bass. '*Penny*', we called it, both because 'P' was for 'Precinct,' and because we house the Penitentiary for the surrounding districts. The bottom few levels, are reserved for maximum security prisoners. The sub-contract for the Max-Sec area of our prison, was awarded to *Velor & Gaston*®. V&G was also the company behind Penny and almost all top-level Security Interface Systems. The web of connections and cross-contracting, amongst all of these corporations, is enough to kill a guy just by thinking about it too long. Bureaucracy was never my thing, and it's the one thing I actually enjoy having 'bots around for. "Penny, pull up the briefing by Investigative Head Curden, Milton-" She cut me off. *"Mr. Curden has not sent in any briefings for you today, Agent Peiler."* 'Odd' was probably an understatement. I made my way to the elevators, at the far end, opposite the entrance.

The reception area was vast but entirely devoid of anything aside from a chest-high wall that looked as if it had grown out of the floor itself, forming a perfectly smooth transition to the lobby desk. No one stood behind it. The doors were also seemingly non-existent until they opened, revealing another seamless transition from one space to another. The elevator was no different. No buttons to denote its position. I arrived at the wall, and waited for the lift. Thinking for a moment about what I had heard at the news stand earlier, "Okay, then pull up all of my files for any missing children across all districts, concentrating on districts 20, A through C, 21, 22A, C, F, and N, 23, and 24B." Jesus fuck, 24B. I didn't know what the IH needed me in for tonight, but I bet it's about these kids.

'You have arrived at the
Eighty-third
floor. Please exist with care!'

"It's not like I'm allowed any other way to live, Penny."

"Don't be so harsh on yourself, Agent. Your Civic Duty is stressful enough as it is on your mortal coil. Now, get out there and face the day!"

Damn, that new AI really puts Psychology to impressive use. Motivation from the Home AI, based on something psychologically relatable to the individual? Now, that was something new. The suicide rates must be spiking again.

Chapter 3

The lift doors opened to an awe-inspiring view of the city, in all its other-worldly glory. The floor disappeared, against a seven-ish metre tall wall of crystal-clear glass. I was on top of the world. I had never been to this office before, and to say that I was paralyzed with wonder is to say the least. *"Agent, please make your way to the left."* She's quite direct.

I turned to notice that the lift continued up and out of sight. I wonder how many floors the Precinct actually has? The elevator shaft and building supports were all part of an island in the centre of the large, ovular, glass room. Or, so I could tell. As I made my way along the illuminated, precipice-presenting hallway, the space suddenly opened up to where the island wall disappeared at a ninety-degree angle to my left, exposing a gorgeous view beyond that I had up to then not been exposed to. This is really how they get you. There were six chairs, shaped like eggs manifesting themselves from the floor, all perfectly fitted at the corner of the office. Five of the chairs were situated in a semi-circle, lining the best spots along the glass wall. The Sixth chair was placed in a way, that all the other five could surround the periphery of the person sitting in the lone chair. I guess I'm supposed to sit there.

The five chairs were facing away from me, as I approached the area. I took my seat. It was comfortable, but, honestly, not as good as my chair back home. These guys may be rich, but that can't buy taste. *'Lo, be it unto me to talk shit whilst living in a glass palace,'* or whatever that crap was, I can't recall where I learned that bit of wisdom. The view was intimidating. The city was all around and bellow me as never before. Usually, a view like this costs a lot of money. I guess it's my lucky day.

Smoothly, the middle chair turns to face me. It revealed that oh-so-fantastic person I love; my boss – Investigative Head of Precinct 21, Milton Fucking Curden. He wore the standard GDC Uniform, which comprised of a slim, form-fitting grey coat with a mandarin collar going up-tight underneath the chin. It came together in a very thin seam down the centre, concealing whatever fastened it together. The coat came down to right above the knee, hugging the frame. The trousers were made of the same grey fabric, and tapered nicely around where the calf meets the ankle. His socks were a void-black, as were his shoes; which had no laces, and were more like a slipper. His skin, was a sickly pale, almost translucent. The flesh clung to his bones, giving a sunken depth to his sullen eyes. Bald, completely. There wasn't a hair on him. Dark rings surrounded his heavily dilated grey-ish eyes. A wide, greasy smile was presented to me, wreathed in cracked, bloody lips. "Johnny," he exhaled through his putrid, yellow-green teeth, gritting and grinding the splintery shafts. Slurping, while running his dripping tongue along the chapped sphincter he called a mouth, he clasped his hands together, hunched over, and leaned forward in my direction. "Johnny, hehe, you know I can't fuckin' stand ya. Hehe, ya know that, right? Right? Hehe, 'course ya do." I looked at him through my shades (I never take them off outside my apartment.) "Hehe, yeah." I replied, making *shooting pistol gestures* with my hands. I'd kill him if the opportunity arose.

"Look, J Money, J Master Flex, look..." he sleazed, "you're a fuck-up, and I'm willing to keep you around, if you're willing to play ball, yeah?" "Are you trying to buy me off, you fucking skin-tube?" I shot back. "Haha, you dumb cunt, you're too stupid to be bought off, I know that. What I want is someone who can work for the guys above me. I thought, if I couldn't get rid of you, I could promote you out of my fucking hair."

"Hilarious joke, you know, about the hair, Milton-"

"SHUT THE FUCK UP! I don't have time for your goddamn fuckery right now Johnathan!" Penny interjected, *"Mr. Curden, you are exceeding your allotted blood-pressure limit covered by the company insurance policy, would you like for me to administer a sedati-"* "Just shoot me up already then!"

-tsssk-

Before I could realize what had happened, a small mechanical arm had appeared from inside the chair, administering a shot to Milton's neck then disappeared back to the interior of the chair. "You have no idea... how good it feels... to surrender control." He slumped back in his chair, sighing, giggling. Licking the drool from the corners of his mouth, he, with great effort, pulled his husk of a form to an upright position. "Alright, you faggot, *-shhllrrppp-* here's the skinny: I need someone to go to the shipping docks in District 20B, and ensure that a container makes it off-world in one piece. There will be another agent assigned to this mission as well. This is Big Company property Johnny; you break it, you buy it." "What's the cargo?" "Hehe, that's above my paygrade, Johnny, don't ask, don't tell." "This isn't a fucking Police assignment Milton, what the fuck is going on here? What's the cargo, who's the company?" Milton leaned back in his chair, grinding his fragmented teeth. "You're asking a lot of questions Johnny. I'd hate for you to ask too many." He sat, drumming his fingers together, glaring at me with those sunken, brown eyes. "Do I take it that you will accept the assignment, and ensure that no criminals make crime of the property?" I'm sure, with the fervor I pursed my face, I created permanent lines in my forehead. "Yeah, sure. What're the details?" I said reluctantly. Hell, the least that could happen is that I find some lead on a bigger case.

"Good, that's good, yes, great in fact, perhaps fucking marvelous. But, who gives a shit, let's talk about the briefing, shall we? Is that *okay* with you, Johnny? *Is it*? You *fucking* prick." Milton's fingers began to twitch wildly, as his eyes darted about the room. "You should lay off that sedative Milt, I heard it causes schizophrenia." "There's no goddamn proof of that, it's all BioDyme® propaganda, meant to hurt 4th quarter sales, so we close out on a fiscal weak note! FUCK! Whatever! Listen retard, tomorrow night, twenty four hours from now, midnight tomorrow, you'll meet Agent 97 at the cargo loading facility outside the *Polaris Major Colonial Space Port*. There, you will go to bay 77-2. Meet with the Deck Captain, he'll tell you what to look out for." I didn't know Curden held stock in Viizor™, BioDyme®'s direct rival, and the producers of the Phyx© sedative. It was a pretty serious market, and it was taking the industry by storm. But, that wasn't the topic of discussion. "This is sketchy as fuck, Milt."

"Do I have to hold your fucking hand through everything, you MILK DRINKER?!" Penny chimed in on cue, *"Mr. Curden, your bloodpressure is once again ri-"* "I SWEAR TO FUCKING GOD! DOSE ME THE FUCK U-" *-tsssk-*

     "You ever see stars in the same way you did as a kid, Johnny?" "To be honest, I don't think I've thought about it, Milton, no. Why?" Milton wrapped his bony fingers around the edges of his egg-chair, giving himself the leverage needed to sit upright again. "Hehe, they make you feel small, Johnny, oh, so small. That's nothing profound, I mean, it might be profound to your backwards ass, but to a decently well-read man like myself..." He motioned to the wall behind me. Inlaid therein was an illuminated, rectangular bookshelf about a metre wide by about half a metre tall. Sitting upon the shelves was a collection of real books; probably twenty-five to thirty of them. "Such a reference would be on the verge of

comical. Do I strike you as a comical man, Johnny?"
What the fuck was this lunatic on about? He must be
high out of his mind on this sedative stuff he's been
OD'ing on lately. Whatever, I really have to do my
job; hate it or not. Who knows, maybe I'll get a
promotion.

"No," I retorted, "no, I don't think you're
comical in the slightest. So, if that's all, I'll meet 97
tomorrow night." I went to get out of my chair. The
creep just grinned a toothy, rotten grin. His chin was
resting on his interlaced fingers, and his elbows upon
his knees. As I turned to make my way back to the
lift, I could feel his eyes piercing into my spine. "Oh,"
- *god dammit* - "and Johnny, don't forget to forget
this meeting, yes? Yes. Hehe, ta'ta for now, J Man."
I'll fucking kill him.

I can't possibly imagine what the hell is going on with this assignment. Since when did our agency ever pull security detail for property shipments? Something wasn't right. Yeah, something was off. The lift ride gave me a bit to think, but still I couldn't shake the feeling that I was walking into something fucked up. "Penny, encrypt my files and have them backed up to drives E and delta12; condition for termination of all files – my death. Upload all of my files to my car's drive, encrypt and hide; access – iris scan." *"Yes, Agent. Is there anything else I can do for you while you are here?"* "Sorry, Penny, I don't think it could work out between us, so, no, there's nothing else I can get from you." I chuckled to myself. *"You have: **ELEVEN** strikes against your Human & Artificial-Lifeforms Resource record, Mr. Peiler. Violations require sensitivity training, in order to be removed from your record. Have a nice day."*

The chilly night air hit my face, only to be blocked as I went to light a cigarette. A long drag; that's what I needed. Livid. Pissed. Seething. I started the walk home. I pulled my collar up around my neck; higher than usual that night. Things seemed a little colder.

Chapter 4

Time is just a highway, and I'm somewhere between salvation and sin. The cherry from my cigarette lit my face, sending a glare off of my glasses. Sure, it was night, probably around eleven PM, but the shades stayed on. Oppressive were the gleaming skyscrapers, draped in neon advertisements. There was no escape, except for on the open road. The vast highway networks that snaked about and connected the concrete metropoli now covering the Earth, were the only real sense of 'freedom' I could conceptualize. There was no reprieve. Hair fluttering in the wind as I roared along in my convertible. The mood visibly changed on my face when her song came on the RadCom™. I turned the volume up and reclined. With an outstretched arm, I played with the wind behind my side mirror. Another drag from this cigarette. Exhaling into the wind above my head, the smoke rose, but was still so far beneath the sound of the roaring engine. "Heh," time *is* but a highway, and I'm just taking a detour.

I think it's clear to say; all life has a beginning, and, therefore must end. However, that does not mean that Existence has no end, for it had no beginning. Inthat, Time has no beginning, and no end. Infinity can only take meaning in the greater scope of all things, and is utterly lost on those things used as fuel for the engines of the cycle of creation and ruination. Maybe I should stop reading? I took a long drag, exhaled, "Haha, ain't no future, like *no future*." The car sailed along the serpentine highway, weaving between buildings, and under bridges, over housing units, and through megaplexes. It was something else. The lights put you in a feeling of traversing the cosmos. You almost forget you're a slave to this place. But hey, that's the job of city planners; to make you forget you're in a city.

Traffic was non-existent at this hour. The endless river of asphalt streamed beneath me, only to be interrupted by the odd red tail-lights I'd swerve to avoid. A shit-eating grin found itself on my face, surprisingly. My foot got a little heavier on the gas. The SpacePort of District 20B was easily an hours drive from the garage I kept my car at, so it gave me time to collect my thoughts. It also gave me enough time to remember that I had shit to do, and waxing philosophic wasn't a good use of my time. "Automota, pull up the files I had transferred to you from Penny." *"John, you know I hate it when you use that show-room title to address me."* "Are you fucking serious right now, *car*?" *"Yeaahh, that's it."* Artificial Intelligence my ass. "When did BMW become BDSM? Pull up the files." What the fuck. I swear, she does it to fuck with me. Listen to me, 'she,' my god, like *it's* a person. I'm losing it.

White light cut my path through the inky blackness of the midnight side-streets, as I neared my destination. I could have taken the nice road all the way to the loading zones, but I wanted to scope the place out a bit first. Considering I got shot at on my way to work, I can't take chances anymore; this city is getting more dangerous by the day. Perfectly, my car fit behind a dumpster. The engine fell silent. "Safety brake on; okay..." I stated, vaulting over the side of my car door, gun in-hand. Neon lights from the city above, cast a tall, dark shadow on the wall adjacent to me as I crept to an outcrop for cover. Drawing my revolver up to my cheek, I leaned to peek around the corner. From my position in the alley, I could see Bay 77-2. Well, at least the back entrance to it. The actual launch site was across the street on the other side of a wall of housing facilities and utility structures. There didn't seem to be an easy way to sneak in. While I was assessing the situation, a glossy, black car pulled up and parked nearest the rear entrance of the bay, across the street from me. Leaning back into the shadows, I could see a man get out and look about. He was dressed in a white button-up shirt, black slacks, and had on a smoke-clear, plastic sports coat. His tie was also black, as were his clunky eye-glasses. What a fucking travesty. The clack of his 'never-seen-the-pavement' shoes, could be heard echoing all around that street. So much for the "best agents." This guy can't be 97. **Shhunk** He couldn't have shut that door any louder. Skittering over to the back door of the hangar like a roach, he appeared to be fiddling with the keypad. Taking note of my surroundings, I presumed the coast to be clear and snuck up behind the guy. "Little late to be alone at the docks, yeah?" Wheeling around like a cyclone, he let out the most high pitched screech that had ever assaulted my ears. His arms were tense to his chest, fists balled up on his face, pushing his ridiculously comical eye-glasses all askew about his head. *"G-GOD FUCK PLEASE DON'T K-KILL ME!!"* escaped his mangled lips. "Are you fucking serious, kid?" "P-please man, l-listen, I d-d-don't have sh-shit on me okay, I-I really can't... Oh, oh shit, y-you must be 88, whew!" A huge sigh deflated him, his body slumping against the wall. "I can't b-believe it's you, Jesus, I thought you w-were a mugger, haha, f-fuck man, that would have b-been som-" I grabbed him up by his collar with my left hand, and with my right, planted the barrel of my gun under his emaciated chin. "If you ever compromise so much information without proper understanding of a situation, I'll liquidate your digits on the spot; get it?!" "Ye-yes-s, c-c-crystal-l..." Putting both the pistol and the poindexter down, I turned to survey the area from this angle. 97 was busy fixing himself, mumbling incoherently.

Curden didn't say anything about a keycode. I wonder what he's up to, if he's splitting info up like this between agents. Must be some seriously top-shelf property. That, or he wants us to think that. *-flick-*

Inhaling deep, I glanced over at the worm I was shackled to on this assignment. "You smoke?" "N-n-" "'Course not; you're a bitch." I exhaled with contempt. Of all the worthless curs I had to deal with at midnight, this one might have been the worst imaginable. "Can you shoot?" "Oh, y-yes, s-sir! I was the t-top sh-shot in my class!" I'm sure he could feel my loathing in his breast, as I glanced over my shoulder at him. Cigarette in mouth, "You mean to tell me, you've never used your weapon on an assignment?" "W-well, n-not exactly, y-you see, I-" "For Christ's sake, just shut up." This guy was going to be the death of me. Oh, well, if shit gets fizzy, I could at least use him as cover. "So," I said, turning toward, and exhaling smoke on 97, "did Curden give you the code for this door?" 97 was having a mini-aneurysm over the cigarette smell, it would seem. "Hey, pencil neck, I'm talking to you. Did Curden give you a code for this door, or are we supposed to enter from another way? You're supposed to be the pointman on this assignment." He looked at me through his coke-bottle glasses. "Oh! R-right, the c-code!" He started to fidget around his clothing, apparently looking for something. "You know, I can see through your coat, and you don't seem to have anything on your person, guy," I snarkily commented, flicking my cigarette butt at his forehead. "H-hey, c-come on, n-now! S-stop f-f-f.." "Fucking with you? Jesus, you'd think with all this technology, they'd fix your speech." "Y-You're a d-dick, man." He was right, I had become some calloused ass of a man over the years. This guy probably didn't deserve my contempt, but it was midnight, and I can't deal with incompetence at this hour. "Alright, maybe I've been a bit harsh, but you need to get your shit together. The world is cruel to guys like you, so fix it, yeah?" He looked over at me with an almost tearful grin. Maybe no one has ever been nice to him, maybe he's as alone as I am. Who knows. But the world was indeed cruel, especially to me. All this suffering wasn't going to come easy to 97, as it never had for myself, nor anyone living in this hell. Unfortunately, he'd either have to pull himself together, or die like so many others. With that said, I need to stop daydreaming about maybe being a good person and helping others, as I have shit to do.

Looking around, I noticed a small alleyway on the side of the loading bay structure. It ran down alongside the adjacent housing units. Practically pitch black down there, aside from a flickering blue light. Classic. I stuck my head into the threshold of the alley, craning my neck about this way and that, trying to get a better read on the place. It smelled of mildew, rot, like any other alley one might weigh heavy on whether or not to venture into. I turned to my right, hands in my pockets, eyebrow raised. 97 was still fumbling about himself, like a woman looking for a spider. Ashes fell from the end of my cigarette, as it bobbed with my lips. "Hey, you comin' or what?" A glint of street-light caught those aquarium-glass spectacles of his, as he looked up at me. His wiry frame, hunched over itself in the half-light of the city night. Like one of those deer caught in headlights that you read about in history stories. "Y-yes-s, s-sir!" He scampered over to where I was, eager and nervous. "O-oh k-kay, l-let's d-do this!" the sound of his voice echoed down the alley, as he drew his service revolver from his hip-holster. "Alright, cowboy, let's see how you're wired." I chuckled.

"So, what's the hold up?" I could hear the knot in his throat move as he swallowed his anticipation. "Y-you mean m-me, me g-go f-first?" "Yes, you. What better way to get used to working in the field, than finding a way into a place we're supposed to be at? The worst that could happen is that we get caught, and are redirected to where we need to be." "H-hey, y-yeah, that's r-right! O-okay, I've got th-this..." "All you, champ." I leaned against the entrance to the alley and went to light another cig.

"Don't worry about me, I've got your back. Go see where this alley leads to, and call back if you find anything. Yeah?" He looked at me, the hesitation slowly creeping back into his face. Before he could scare himself out of moving again, "Hey, listen, just go, or I'll shoot you myself, yeah?" "Y-yeah, r-right, I g-got it." He gripped his pistol with both hands, holding it low, and began inching his way down the alley. About fucking time.

Good kid or not, he'll never make it in this world. This job will grind his bones, and crush his weak soul. I almost feel bad for him. "H-hey!" came a faint cry, echoing down the alley. Without shifting off the wall, I glanced down the dark passage. There he was, jumping up and down like a madman. "I-it l-leads this w-way!" Great, I guess I have to get up. And so I did, hands in my pockets, cig in my mouth, shuffling down the alley. I leaned my head all the way back to look up, between the towering structures.

Wires and pipes ran every which way, water dripped from so many surfaces that it appeared to be raining. Oh, this dreary, lonely alley, equipped with its own rain to remind me, that no matter where I am, I'll always be getting pissed on by this fucking city.

"So, what did you find?" I asked as I approached. He was standing at a T-junction. "L-look! It l-leads d-down to the l-launch b-bay! I think..." blurted 97, pointing to what would be the right fork. I looked left. It was darker down that way. Flickering lights, leaking pipes; shady. "Take note of your surroundings." My eyes darted all around as I gave 97 the advice. "Alright, look, follow me, look out behind us, don't get trigger happy." I drew my weapon and proceeded to go down the path leading to the launch bay. Only the soft clop of shoes on wet cement could be heard against the cold silence of this urban trench. We rounded a bend in the alley to discover two figures standing in a doorway.

"GDC, don't obstruct our business," I muttered as I passed, gun clearly visible. "Woah-ho-ho there big fella, what's the heat for, yeah? Yeaaahh," spewed the mullet-punk, as he tore himself from an equally repulsively dressed female. "Yeah mista', what's the big deal, can't nobody have any damn privacy?" she squeaked. "You're in a fucking alley, you goons, now beat it before I clock your digits and chalk it up to gang violence." I didn't even turn to look back at them. "Oh, yeah, you got some nerve *bro*, might need to teach you a lesson. Or maybe your bitch here can get it first..." The sounds of a switch-blade opening and a heavy metal object hitting the ground rang through the night. "Oh, fucgg..." I turned to see that 97 had been pinned against the wall by the neon-urchin, knife at his throat. The kid had dropped his fucking gun. "Hehe, yeaah..." Licking his lips, the thug leaned in close to 97. "You got the circuitry, pig? Nah, I fuckin' doubt it." "Put him down punk, or I'll shoot your lady friend..." I raised my pistol to cover

53

the frame of the woman standing in the doorway. "Now... now hold on mista,'" she had managed to form herself to the doorframe in sheer terror. "If you fuckin' point that shit at her, I'll..." the punk dropped 97 for an instant, and turned his knife towards me. "Bad move." Like lightning, I reoriented my firearm, and unloaded six rounds of hot lead. His body contorted; blood spattered, and in an agonizing scream he toppled to the ground with an awful heaviness – dead. "OH MY GOD!! NOOOOOOO!!!" the villainess flung herself onto the limp corpse of her lover. A devastated, sobbing wreck, she turned to me. "How could you?! You fucking monster! I'll kill you!!" Springing to her feet, she leapt at me, covered in blood and tears. I could see the hatred in her bloodshot eyes. She was upon me; baring her teeth, saliva frothing, hands outstretched like claws – *BANG* – red mist peppered my face. Before I could react, the full weight of my body in motion hit the ground like a train.

Chapter 5

The rain was a refreshing element to my night on second thought. It gave me a slight reprieve in an otherwise torrid situation. There was a great weight on my chest. I laid there in the rain for a moment. Did she shoot me? Am I dead? I looked down towards my chest. Her body was on top of mine, and with some grunting I managed to heave it off of me. Getting up onto my knee, I caught my breath. I looked around. 97 was standing not far from the guy I shot a moment ago, gun in-hand, shaking like a leaf in a storm. "I-... I-... I-is sh-she dead?" I looked over at the woman. "Yeah, yeah, I think you killed her." Sighing, I stood up. "Good shot." "I... I..." He couldn't stand straight. "Hey, kid, what's wrong?" I exclaimed, walking over to him. "It'll be okay, it's always tough your first time. You saved my life, probably, so, thank you." He remained emotionless as I patted him on the shoulder. Leaving him to deal with himself, I set about trying to identify the punks we had just slaughtered in an alley.

"Let's see here, *Dillon Hannon*, 27, civic digits... 65-43-85. Nothing impressive," I muttered to myself, standing up after searching the guy I shot. Shame, he was so young. Just wasn't his lucky day. Taking a cigarette out of my pack, I looked over to the other mangled heap. Water, dripping from the lattice of pipes and wires above, had merged with the flowing blood to create a small river weaving over and down the uneven alley floor. I walked over to the girl. Standing over her corpse made me stop and think for a moment. She looked innocent. Almost majestic. Eyes wide open; frozen in the time of her demise. Mouth slightly open, with only a small trickle of blood to mar the pristine image of her now-pale lips. Porcelain features outlined a face devoid of blemish, standing stark, against the watered-down pool of crimson that had gathered beneath her frail head. Her left hand was arranged in such a way, as to accentuate her face. Lying there curled up, she almost appeared to be asleep, if not for the open eyes.

Dark crimson-coloured hair, once strawberry-blonde, covered the gaping wound in the back of her skull. I shuddered. Getting down on one knee, I reached over to sift through her jacket pockets. Upon hearing the shuffling of feet, "So, you've finally come to, huh?" Peering over my shoulder, I saw 97 standing near the girl's legs by the wall we first found the two against. He was shaking visibly. "Put your gun away before you accidentally discharge it," I huffed. "88, I-... I-is she g-going t-t-t..." "*To live*? Wow, that's some serious denial. Not a chance; you might, however, have a *shot* at being a brain surgeon." I chuckled. "No ID. Fuck." "D-does s-s-she have a b-b-barcode?" stuttered the barely recovered 97. I grabbed her left arm, and upon doing so, shifted the body in a way that tilted the head back. The mess of what once was her most advanced organ spilled out into the gutter along with a fresh torrent of blood. Almost no heaving sounds preceded the geyser of vomit that escaped 97. "AAAAHHHH GODDD!!" was blurted out inbetween puke spasms. "No barcode. She's not 18 yet." I stood up swiftly. Loading another six rounds into my revolver, I marched over to the degenerate that ate the last six. Searching for something, I turned up empty. No markings, no cards, no gang paraphernalia, nothing. This was something serious, I knew this was related to the missing kids, I just fucking knew it. But I couldn't prove it. "97, come on, we have to get to the Loading Bay, we're already late." Taking mental notes of everything, I trudged along down the alley.

Eventually, we came upon a narrow exit to the launch pads. It was blocked by a large chain fence that went up about three stories. "Whelp, that's a bitch." "I c-can't c-climb that," said 97, looking up at the intimidating barrier. "Yeah, me neither, kid." I chuckled while reaching into my interior coat pocket. "W-w-what's that?" came a confused inquiry from over my shoulder. "This, my boy, is a laser cutter.

And..." I got down on the ground. "It's our ticket into this place." Tracing a small semi-circle out of the chain, I fashioned us an entrance. "W-Wow, w-where did y-you get i-it?" "Don't ask questions." I put the device back in my pocket and made my way through the cut-out.

It was a spectacular sight to behold. The city opened up into a massive, flat plane. Surrounded on all sides by towers and spires exalted in neon lights of every colour, the Space Port gave off an air of the religious. A cult of lights and iron. A rocket was taking off in the distance, far across the vast plateau. Brilliant blue and white fire ejected from its thrusters to push it ever upward towards the heavens. To where, I'd never know. Some colony I'd never see; some planet I'd never visit. I wasn't destined for such things. Oh, well. I took another drag from my cigarette.

Alright, so, just over here to the right of us should be Hangar 77-2. I walked on, following my keen sense of direction. Sure enough, there were the giant block numbers, **7 7 − 2**; done in now-chipped black paint, on once-white rusted, sliding doors. The hangar doors were immense, easily over a hundred and fifty metres tall. The lighting was as daylight at high-noon, casting almost no shadows in the hangar at all. Peeking around, I noticed the hangar was empty aside from some maintenance scaffolding and a narrow catwalk, which skirted the third floor perimeter of the back wall and both sides of the mega structure. Where was everyone? I guess this is as good a place as any to make a shady exchange. "97, look around for a deck captain, should be wearing some kind of corporate uniform, probably Æromark™. So, look for the red circle with the white rocket." 97 nodded in compliance, and sauntered off to the far left side of the hangar while I proceeded to the right. The bay-centre was barren until you reach the back, aside from that scaffolding and a few work benches and kits. Definitely usable cover if I found myself out there, but nothing really caught my notice.

Creeping along the right wall of the hangar, I kept my eyes peeled for any movement, any sign of life. As I neared the back of the bay, I noticed that the wall carefully concealed a few large cargo doors, painted to match the rest of the facade. Whose bright idea was this? Whatever. I needed to find the deck captain, and I'm sure he's in this building somewhere...

*** BEEEP ** BEEEP ** BEEEP ***

My musing was cut short by a safety siren. The doors I had just come upon began to open, swinging wide. "Alright, loading team follow me, we're taking shipment 443 to the edge of the tarmac," came a voice from the now-revealed interior of the facility. A large loader smoothly crept past the threshold of the cargo doors. I stood back along the wall, partially covered by the open door. I'd wait to see what all emerged before I started flashing my badge around. *I can see why these are considered Centipedes*, I thought, looking at the machine; *with all the wheels, and how slow it is*. Most all of the fuzzy-animals may have died off long ago, but there's always a bug around to crawl up your ass. The red colour of the vehicle let me know it was Æromark™ property; they're the only ones that use this much red. The loading bed was filled with crates all stamped with CryoCom® insignia; stacked, ready for transport. CryoCom® dealt mostly in cryogenic freezing of biological matter for long-distance travel in space. Or to preserve something that is unconscious or in stasis. Which begs the question: what was the cargo? Was that even the shipment I was looking for?

Following it, were a few dock hands in red overalls and hard hats; five by my count. I was about to follow after them but heard more footsteps. Four burly dudes came out after them. Black military-style uniforms, shades, armed with heavy weapons. Bald, all of them. I leaned out from my crevice for a better look. Barcodes on the base of their skulls, right where the neck meets the head. Androids. What the fuck did Curden send us into? He didn't say shit about Andro's, nothing at all about this kind of security, I thought *we* were the security? Stumbling about after them, was a strange little man wearing a pink suit, styled in the same fashion as Curden's sleek get up. He was holding what I assumed to be a manifest and digipad. Looking at one, then the other, then at his feet; he continued to trip over himself, trying desperately to look at his notes and keep up with the cadre ahead of him. This was my guy, it had to be. "You look a little nervous, pal." I emerged from my spot. He turned on his heel with a gasp. Sharp, crooked, and hooked; his nose jutted out from his face, like the proboscis of some blood-sucking insect. His teeth were bucked, like a fucking rodent, chattering and sniveling, wagging his tongue as he did. They were as yellow as rodent's teeth too. Bulbous lips, glistened with drool in the sun-like lighting, framed with fat cheeks covered in a wispy beard. It was almost picturesque. He stared at me through tiny circular spectacles. "Are you from GDC?" he said with a heavy Xio accent. "Yes." I approached him slowly. "Oh, gawd, ya're late, ya need ta check deez pape's and sign he-a for da ca'go maneefest and deez documents need ta be signed aswell and-" "Man, listen, your shitty little voice is giving me a migraine and you aren't breathing when you speak, chill the fuck out. It's late at night, and I'm not in the mood for your nonsense. What am I here for, what did Curden need us to do?" I calmly interjected, sauntering up to him. "C-Curden sent ya, huh? Where's da other GDC guy den?"

He must mean 97. I looked around for him, but didn't see him. He could easily be hiding behind all of this heavy machinery and personnel that just made an entrance. Not wanting to give up the ghost if I didn't have to regarding whether I knew 97, "I don't know, I'm sure he's around here somewhere, why?" "He needs ta sign deez. Yous need ta wait for da next shipment ta come t'rough, den we can tawlk." So quickly did he waddle his short ass off to catch up to the convoy on its way to the launch sites, that unknowingly his little pink matching hat flew off. It landed on the floor behind him. Picking it up, I noticed how strange a hat this was, it practically serves no useful purpose. Oh, well. I'll give it back to that fat piece of shit when I see him again, maybe I can get a reward. I chuckled audibly, and proceeded to search the other side of the hangar for 97.

Xiotron©®™℠; they own it all, and if they don't, they own stock in it, or you're in debt to them, or you pay rent to them... You get my drift. Never, not once, have I had a pleasant interaction with a Xio. Money-obsessed, greedy, power-hungry; nothing good. Luckily, they don't like anyone else either, so they keep things quick when they need to interact with us. But, mulling over groups of hominids I despise won't help me find 97. I'll think about big money and bad business later, for now I'm on the job. I could really use a cigarette, too bad these hangars are all equipped with those heat detection systems that'll flood this bitch with foam so quick we'd all suffocate before we knew what happened. Not a fate I care to meet. If I'm getting smothered, it's gonna be better than that; ha, I can worry about spending the rent on a good time later. Jesus, who am I anymore?

I motioned my head in a jerking manner to get the hair out from in front of my shades. Where the fuck is he? Walking over to some work benches, at the far end of the hangar in the corner, sounds began to reach my ears coming from my intended destination. I could see someone moving about behind them so I approached cautiously. With the muzzle of my pistol peeking around the edge of the cluster of benches first, I leaned around to see what was making the commotion. 97 was bound and gagged on the floor, with a nasty gash on his forehead which was spilling blood all over his face. "Jesus fuck!" I exclaimed without control, moving in to untie him. "What the fuck hap..?!" *Oh, right, he's gagged.* I pulled the gag from his mouth and 97 began heaving, and gasping for air. Choking on himself, he rolled over onto his stomach, giving me a better handle on untying the knots keeping him roped up. "Th-th-they f-f-f-fuck-cking hit me!" "No shit. What happened, who did this?" Sitting up and massaging his face and aching parts, "I-it w-was somewuh-one, I didn't s-s-see him-m. He came f-from behind." "And he's got your gun," I stated, looking over the benches we were crouched behind; maybe I could see something. *There*! On the catwalk, on the same side of the hangar we were on, almost directly above us, a figure stood, watching, lurking. I leaped up, pointing my weapon towards the intruder, shouting, "GDC! Drop your weapon and-" ***BRRRRRTT*** — A burst of automatic gunfire peppered the cloaked individual, spraying the walls and catwalk with crimson. Two of the Androids had opened fire and were moving in to inspect the area. "H-holy shit!" "Keep down kid, something ain't right." As soon as the words left my lips, a massive explosion tore the cargo loader in twain, sending pieces of flaming metal and all sorts of debris flying in all directions, as it was leaving the hangar. I covered my head and ducked behind the iron work benches. The shockwave knocked everything that wasn't tied down off its shit.

Everything in the hangar entrance was aflame, including the crew and a few deckhands who were wildly thrashing about, screaming to their mothers in the final moments of their miserable lives.

The flames were of such intensity, that it melted the flesh from the bones of those poor men unfortunate enough to get caught by the blast. If I were closer, I'd put them out of their misery, but I don't think they can live long like that anyhow. Slumping to the ground, one by one, they dropped to their knees, falling face first into a puddle of their own liquefied being. I was enraptured by their pitifulness; their descent into the abyss of fire, agony, smoke, misery, ash, and sorrow. Their gore, bubbling on the floor about their charred husks, turned black as it became hard in the likeness of lava once it has cooled. 97 was curled into a ball, holding his ears, shaking uncontrollably - I think he pissed himself. I could barely make sense of what was happening, then my haze was shattered by cracks of machine-gun fire from all directions. Bullets went whizzing past, ricocheting off every other surface between the entrance and the back wall of the hangar. I stopped to think where the foam extinguisher was, and why I wasn't dead from suffocation yet either. Someone must have disabled the system, but that would mean... fuck.

I crouched behind the benches, peering over the side, careful not to be spotted. There they were, sure enough, militants of some sort. Terrorists? What the fuck is this about? What kind of cargo is this, that these guys want it so bad? Is this a robbery? A jail break? A kidnapping? I had no idea, but the bullets that were flying kept reminding me that I didn't have time to think about it. The Androids were battling it out over the hangar bay and loader wreckage against a force of black-clad militants that had no discernable numbers, but there were at least ten of them near the loader. I had a clear shot at them. They were using this side of the ruined loader as cover, against the Androids that were concentrated on the right side of the hangar. I didn't see that cretin of a deck captain anywhere either. Not wanting to draw attention to myself, I looked around for another way to get to the loading doors, at the back of the hangar. They were still open, but that was a long, open run to get there from where we were hiding. Regardless, we needed to get out of this situation that we were clearly not prepared for. My revolver wasn't going to do shit against their military-grade stuff; essentially, we were fucked.

If 97 knew we were fucked, he'd probably suck-start his pistol right here. Luckily it was stolen. I needed to convince him to chance this escape, as it might be our only opportunity before more show up and take our position. "Hey, they're distracted by the Androids, we need to make a break for it. Get up!"

"Y-ye-" "Shut up! Just follow my lead!" We crouched around the back side of the benches, getting as far from the terrorists and as close to the doors as possible. God, that's a long run. "Alright, on three." "W-wh-" "One!" I harshly stated.

"Two!" I looked over toward the door, then at the battle, then at 97. I saw untold fear in his eyes. He was looking directly at me, shaking, perspirating, teeth clenched, fists balled.

"Three!" We bolted for the cargo entrance. 97's new shoes were slipping on the slick hangar floor, making it hard for him to keep up. I'm sorry, kid.

I took off as fast as I could. "Today! is not! the fucking! day!" huffing as I went. Rounds pinged off the catwalk above me, the wall off to my left, the floor... I felt the hot, yet cold touch of an unbearable piercing pain strike through my left calf.

I put my hands out to block my uncontrollable fall to the ground at break-neck speed. This was it. I was going to die in a fucking terror attack on a shady job I shouldn't have been involved with. What a way to close out the story of my life. I started crawling to the door, dragging my left leg as I went. Keeping as low to the ground as I could, I turned to look at the scene evolving at the flaming wreckage, near the hangar entrance. The terrorists were seemingly leaving, but why? Was help coming? A few of them had been killed, it looked like, and some were attempting to drag their comrades bodies away under heavy duress. I looked back to my desired destination and began crawling again. The clapping of fast-moving shoes was quickly coming up behind me. "Y-you f-fuck-cking prick! S-serves you r-right!" "Thanks for the lecture, kid, gimme a hand, yeah?" I threw my arm up towards him, and he helped me to my feet. "Thanks, now let's get the fuck gone." We began making our way to the cargo doors, it wasn't far now.

By the time we reached the doors, the militants had cleared out. A few new Androids came in from outside and two showed up from inside the building. One approached us as we came up to the door. *"You are not authorized to enter this facility without the proper-"* I flashed my badge, and the andro turned and walked away. God, I hate those things. "I-if we had j-just stayed, y-you'd be f-fine." He grinned. Shaking my head, I used 97 as a crutch as we entered the building's interior. To the left were a few crates and a desk, with a Holoviewer™ on the wall above it. Under the desk was that sniveling rat deck captain. "Hey! You didn't say shit about this, and neither did Curden! What the fuck is going on?!" shouting as we approached, I had just about had it. "Look, I'm just as surprised as yous, yeah? C'mon, I had nuttin' on it, honest, cross my heart," came the mousy squeaks from under the desk. He began to crawl out from under his shelter. "I'm assumin' dey're gone?" He looked past us at an Android that had just walked in. It nodded in assurance. "Good, now, let's finish our business." "Look, pal, you corporate fucks have been jerking my chain for too long; I want answers-" "Yous can't afford 'em, now, shut ya fuckin' mout', sign da fuckin' documents, an' dis nightmare is ove'. For all of us." Glaring at him, I outstretched my arm, motioning with my hand for him to give up the manifest. He placed it in my hand, grinning widely, making his face even more pointy than it already was, his triangular ears wiggling with excitement. I looked at it, then back at him. There were spaces for five signatures, three of which were already printed. I was the fourth, and I guessed that the fifth is the flight crew. The one above my place, read the name *Seinman*, which I assumed was my pudgy friend here. I put my thumb on the Esig© to confirm my authorization of the crate, which I had never seen, to be flown off world. I had apparently performed an inspection of this cargo, and all they needed was my signature. "I need ya'rs too... Dat's a good boy..." The fat, yet bony, fingers of the Xio pointed to another Esig© on another manifest, indicating that 97 had also performed an inspection. 97 complied. "Dat'll be all, gents. Hehe, see ya 'round." With that, the Xio waddled off into the depths of the facility. He stopped, and turned for a moment. "Oh, an' ya can let ya'selves out down dat hallway, leads ta da back alley ya vermin parked ya shit-mobile in." With a wheezy chuckle, he turned to leave again. "Hey, you forgot your hat, dick." I tossed his little round hat to him. Throwing his hands up to shield himself from the projectile, he let out a mincy squeal. Pathetic. "Now you can turn your back on me."

I almost inhaled the entire cig in one go. I was slumped against the wall, next to the door we couldn't get into earlier. What a fucking night. I looked over at 97, who was sitting on the hood of his car, staring at the ground, kicking his left foot back and forth ever so slightly. "Pretty fun for your first assignment, yeah? Haha." Nothing but silence. Something I've grown to expect from everyone and everything. "You'll get used to it." "W-we need to g-get you to a h-h-hospital, man." The kid was right, I was bleeding pretty bad. "You don't look too good either, kid. Let's get that head looked at while we're at it." He reached up to touch his forehead, then nodded in agreement. "Alright, help me to my car, luckily it's my left leg, so I can drive still. Follow me, make sure I don't pass out and crash, yeah?" "Y-yeah."

"Johnny, baby, what did they do to you?!" "Automota; set up an emergency hospital visit at the usual clinic in 20C-" *"Johnny, that's almost an hour away!"* "Then let's step on it." 97 was standing next to my car, blinking with one eye then the other. "Y-you have an o-odd relationship with y-your c-c-c-" "Yeah, I know. Just follow me." He went to leave. "And kid," I shouted after him, "thanks again."

Chapter 6

Squinting my eyes, I peered through the haze of smoke lingering about my head. The cigarette cherry slowly burned, only increasing the smog in my apartment. He was the only person, other than her, to ever sit in that chair. Sporting a classic fu-manchu moustache and his long, white hair in a tight top-knob; he looked like a kung-fu master, a regular sifu. Had a black robe and everything. Total, fucking, badass; and that's me saying that. Stroking his wispy beard, "约翰，您需要练习耐心。" Exhaling, I looked

(Yuehan, nin xuyao lianxi naixin.)

over at him. "I know. I know, next time I'll just wait to see if they kill me, Wu-chin, great fucking plan-" "You don' have'a pran, John! No pran, no hope'a success. Why you no read da PDF I give you? Sun-Tzu is'a no foor, John." He was right, I was getting wrestless, impatient. "Haha! First you must eat'a *Nü-dL®,* or no strength to save ci-ty. Hahaha," Laughing heartily and clapping, he rocked back and forth in my chair. Crazy old man.

83

Popping a box of *Nü-dL*® open, I reached around my bed for a fork. "Here! Haha, what man has no chop'a sticks? Heheh." He tossed a small bundle at me. The chopsticks were enclosed in some kind of leather, tied together with twine. Hand-carved by the looks of them. I'd admire them later, when I wasn't doped up on pain-meds and nicotine. "Wu, I'm running low on Orbit™. PlanetCide© flavour, if you get a choice. You know I'm good for-" "We go over dis awr'da time; I know you are an honest man. But, dat shit'a gon' keer you, John. Drink'a tea-" With noodles hanging from my mouth, I used the chopsticks to point to a tea-stash by the *Food*'Oh'*Matic*®. "You expect me to berieve you drink'a Ear'r Grey? Is'a piss-watah!" We had a healthy chuckle. "You ever rocate d'ose missing chirdren?" It hits heavy, when the only person you respect asks you a question, and you know you have to disappoint them with the answer. Looking over at him, "No. No, I haven't found anything."

"She berieved you curd do it, dat you curd do some good in dis ci-ty. I, arso berieve in you, John." He stroked his beard. I poked at the food in my take-out box with the chopsticks. What do you say to that? Nodding, I continued eating. "Rook, Johnny, rook, I'm'a you. Hahah!" Looking up I saw Wu-chin wearing my shades, making odd faces. He always knew how to cheer me up. We laughed and talked until I passed out from the RinoKane©. It's a pretty good pain-killer, and it works really fucking well when you blow rails of it off the dash of your car.

Having a day off was pretty nice. Four, however, that was otherworldly. But tomorrow it was back on the clock. A long sigh escaped me as I exhaled, "You're probably sick of me already, aren't you?" "Meowww..." "Yeah, that's what I figured, you and every other woman that's ever spent two days straight around me. Except one..." The cat leapt into my lap, purring and kneading as she did. Petting her with one hand, I poured myself a shot with the other. Droplets of water slowly streamed down my window, reflecting the city's neon-lights in all different directions; like tiny jewels, falling in the night. God, I love this chair.

The pain was bearable, and I could walk decently after my recovery time. I stood up to gaze out over the run-down hellscape that was my district. Grimy shit-hole. It was only about five PM, but already the skies were pitch black. They normally were dark all day, what with all the pollution from the factories; spires of industry, spewing a deadly miasma of toxins like a blanket over the worthless drones that keep the fires coked. I was no exception. My ruminating was cut short when a soft knocking broke the silence. Pistol in hand, I went to look through the peep-hole. With a sigh of relief, and disbelief, I could make out those ridiculous glasses, and that greasy, slick hair: 97. Opening the door,

"How did you find me?" I stated, grabbing him by the arm and dragging him in quickly. "I-I, uh…" "Shut up." I peered into the hallway, looking to see if there was anyone else. "Were you followed? Shit, like you'd know. Well, you're here now, and I don't think I can stomach listening to you babble without another shot of liquor," I grumbled under my breath, as I went for another drink. *-flick-* Exhaling into the air as I sat deep into my chair, I turned to look at 97. "Sit on the bed if you want, I'm sure you're cleaner than it is." I motioned. "Th-thanks." He sat down, hands clasped together in his lap, legs together, very rigid. "Are you hungry or something? Want some *Nü-dL®*?" He shook his head slightly, side to side. "So…" My eyes darted towards him. "Are you going to tell me why you're in my apartment?" "W-well, I'm-m supposed to b-b-be your new p-part-t-" "Partner?!" I exclaimed, sitting up straight. "Look kid, I'm not supposed to be on the clock until tomorrow, why couldn't this nonsense wait?" "B-b-because I th-think Curden is up t-to something. Last n-night was s-sket-tchy." I had to hand it to him, he had good instincts.

Lighting another cig, "Yeah... Yeah, I can't say I disagree with your gut on this one, kid." "B-but how will we e-ever find out? H-he's too p-p-powerful." "We need evidence that the Judges can't refute. And I think I may know a lead to start with. Are you armed?" 97 shook his head, glancing down at his hip. "Heh, surprised they're taking so long to replace it." Getting a quick stretch in before I stood up, I grabbed my pistol off the desk and holstered it. "After our last bit of fun together, nothing should be an issue for you; not everyone survives a flash warzone unarmed, you know?" I exhaled, walking towards the door. "Wh-where are we g-" "Follow me, I'll explain on the way."

Shutting the door behind us caused an echo to reverberate down the hall. Making our way to the elevator, I could hear the click of heels around the corner. Great. As we came into the T-way at the elevators, my ears were accosted by that familiar, squeaky voice. "Hey, Johnny, heading out for the night? Want some company?" "Actually, Tracy, I *could* use your company tonight." Turning to her, I smirked, raising one eyebrow above my shades. "Wait, really? Okay! What kinda suck were yo-" "Not any of that you nickel-slot slut; I need arm candy to not look suspicious walking into *Maze*™ with only this shab." I motioned to 97. Tracy leaned back into a contrapposto pose, eyeing up the skinny kid behind me. "W-wait, where a-are w-w-" "Oh, he's cute, Johnny, they'll eat him alive in that part of town." "That's what passes for cute?" My eyes rolled over to look at 97, standing there with his hands in his pockets, tapping at the floor with his shoe. Is he shy? He can't possibly think this thing is hot. Whatever.

"Look, Tracy, I need you to come with us. I may need access to the club and two unaccompanied guys aren't getting in, not without serious money or clout. How's about it?" She looked around for a moment, opened her small handbag, closed it. "Yeah, alright. Not like I'm doin' anything else." '*Ding*' We all boarded the lift as the doors opened.

Leaning against the back of the elevator as I customarily did, I paused my mind to analyze the dynamics being cultivated by my new-found cadre of misfits. Tracy was standing contrapposto to my left, as she's programmed to do. Always wearing the same turquoise faux-fur get-up, with those fucking bright orange shoes to match her artificially neon hair. She took a pair of black, thin, pointy cat-eye sunglasses out of her purse and donned them. The rims lit up with an orange LED strip. What a fucking mess. 97 was hunched in the corner to my right; his shoulders forming a sort of prison around his weak frame as he sunk ever deeper into himself. He kept making darting glances at Tracy, as if he'd never been this close to a woman before, or even a machine that looks like one. Explains a lot. *'Ding'* Disembarking the lift, we made for the streets. Looking around at the crowded streets, "My car is a couple blocks from here, I'll explain when we hit the road; you never know who is listening around here."

Rain-soaked tarps hung over the makeshift market stalls littering the streets around us. Every fucking step I took, I could smell a different urban urchin that had been wallowing in their own shame and filth for too long. The deformed faces of the gutter trash inhabiting this place could scare the dead. Every dysgenic creature imaginable made this wretched city their home... and we were going to a worse part than this. We came to the Block 13 Garage, where I kept the vehicle. It was just a fucking warehouse, but hey, it beats parking on the street.

"Gimme a sec..." escaped my lips as I went towards the security entrance. Leaving the others outside, I went into the main office. Opening the door revealed a sterile tile room, bereft of life. It was entirely empty except for a kiosk in the centre and a door on the opposite side. The wall across from me, that contained the other door, was made of thick glass. This allowed all the 'poors' who couldn't afford a nice car to gawk at all the fancy models like kids in a toy-shop. The only thing that caught my eye today, was that it looks like the prick above me on the 75th floor finally got that *Kestir©* he wanted. Piece-a' shit looks like a dong. Uncontrollably, I laughed aloud, "It's even in beige, HAHA!"

* Bing * Bong *

The comm system kicked on. *"Making fun of other motorists vehicles again, I see, Mister Peiler?"* came a very posh, gentlemanly voice. "If they didn't buy shit, they wouldn't get shit." *"You are quite the tart, Mister Peiler, certainly one for the ages. Now, if you are finished amusing yourself at the expense of others for free, would you kindly retrieve your vehicle. And will you be requiring any services today: petrol, perhaps?"* I had to think for a sec. "Yeah, top 'er off, Vince." *"As you wish, sir."*

Bright red paint trimmed in chrome, white wall tires with spoke wheels, white canvas top with matching interior. Yeah, she was the shit. It's the only lady I need in my life. She's got all the curves I need, and damn does she scream when I lay into 'er. 7-Litre TurboMaxRev®, fossilfuel injected V10 fat-body on a nanoframe chassis. And, yes, in case you're wondering, I do live in a shit-hole just so I can revel in the privilege of driving this god-tier auto-boner.

Automota, was a BMW™ Walkyrie Klasse© *EEE* Roadster; and she was my piece of the pie.

I walked through the door in the glass wall to enter the showroom. Down the aisle I walked, passing car after car until... Yeah, there she is. Smirking, I put a cig up to my lips and lit it, taking a heavy drag. Exhaling, as I approached the driver door, "You ready for some action, baby?" The door opened for me to get in. "Hey, don't get fresh, you ever think that maybe I like vaulting over the door, rather than opening it?" It makes me look cool, I know that, but the car doesn't need to program my social insecurities into its AI. And I have no idea why they made her voice so sultry and seductive, but damn, does it just make it weirder. *"Well, why don't you ever say anything?"* "Why do you ever say anything?" *"This is why you're single John; get in. Ya' always got me though... rawr."* Another day in paradise.

Sliding my thumb over the ignition verification, I couldn't help but tingle at the anticipation of what was about to happen next...

BBBVVVVVVRRMMMMM

I was harder than diamonds.

Pulling out into the street, my two companions approached me like a couple-a' hookers. Well, one actually was, so that's fitting. As they reached me, I flipped the switch for the roof to retract. "Oh, come on, Johnny, you're going to fuck my hair up before we get to the club? Come the fuck on..." bitched Tracy as she rolled her eyes demonically far into her skull. Muttering under my breath, "Who gives a fuck." I motioned for 97 to sit shotgun. "Tracy, plop your plastic ass in the back." "*So, who're your friends? They better not be filthy, Vince just washed me and...*" "Oh, so Vince is coming for my spot?" "*At least he cleans my pipes, you tease.*" 97 opened the door and got in, looking all around in awe. I knew he envied this rig, who didn't? She was the hottest car on the road. The neon robo-slut climbed in the back, and reclined in the bench-style seat. "This is really comfy Johnny, I didn't know you were a man of taste. What a girl wouldn't give to have this pick her up at the club, I mean it would-" "Switch off, Tracy." My hand cranked the volume dial with haste. (Yeah, that's right, retrofitted analog dials.) The roar of the engine, and Judas Priest®, exploded through the city streets as I pealed out; foot like a lead brick.

Chapter 7

"S-so, where are w-we-" "Remember that creepy deck captain?" I interjected. 97 nodded in agreement. "When I mentioned Curden, he recoiled and fumbled a bit, which made me believe he either fears Curden, or fears who would have sent Curden. Anyway, I wanted to know what he was up to, so when he dropped his hat, I picked it up and returned it to him, yeah?" "Y-yeah, I rem-m-member, mhmm." "I put a tracking device in the hat, and for the past few days in recovery, I've been watching where he's been going. He's all over the place, but the one place he goes every night, after he's done running around, but before he goes back to his comfy pad in 20A1, is this location, — Automota, put it on the radio communicator— it's the *Maze*™ Club, here in 20C." I pointed to the GPS map and notes on the screen in the car's centre console. "I don't know what he does there, or who he meets or reports to, but he always goes there for at least two hours, usually between five to seven PM. We're going to find out what he knows about what was in those crates we sent off world." 97 looked around at the city whizzing by, then back at me. "S-so why do w-we n-need her? We're G-GDC, we c-can g-go question anyone." "Anyone *except* people with authority over GDC, and I suspect that if we go into this place badges blaring, we'll spook any leads in the building. And if that little Xio is working for Curden, or whatever their arrangement is, it'll tip them off that we're on to them; and the crooks go further under-ground." Nodding in understanding; 97 sat quietly, hands clasped in his lap, legs together, eyes forward. "Th-this is a n-nice car you have h-here. I-I c-couldn't get a g-good l-look the other n-night," he stammered. *"Hey there, what's your name?"* I knew she'd reply before I did. "Hey, *Car*, stop chatting up the kid..." *"If you keep acting like a dick, Johnny, I'll fucking kill us both!"* The bucket of bolts in my backseat piped up, "Uh oh, Johnny boy, looks like you pissed off your lady friend..."

"Switch off, Tracy!" *"Switch off, Tracy!"*

Not long into the now-silent part of our drive, I kept glancing over at 97, realizing that he was staring at me. He probably wasn't blinking either. After a while, I couldn't stand it any longer. "Hey, kid, seriously, are you in love with me or something? What the fuck is wrong with you?" His eyes got wide, and he started fidgeting. "N-no, I'm n-not g-g-gay, I was j-just wondering, when we'd d-discuss being p-part-" Without looking at him I interrupted, "No. I don't do 'Partners.'" "B-but Curden s-said..." "Fuck that wacko. Do you honestly think I give a rat's ass about whatever-it-is that Curden wants? No." The wind blew over us in the cool night air, soaring down the highway. "W-well, I'm H-Harold Flynn." "No, you're 97." I couldn't tell him that every time I had a partner they got snuffed out by some unfortunate twist of fate, but I couldn't let him live in ignorance either. "Look, I've lost a lot of partners, three names, and more numbers than I can count. You aren't going to be the fourth name." He looked at me, then at the road, then down at his feet. It was a harsh thing to tell the kid; that I didn't even want to know his name. But it was better for both of us.

I never talk about my past much, why should I? It fucking sucks. This job is practically all I know, and with it, all the woes and shit that come with such a life. Thinking about the faces of the past, all the hate, violence, depravity; good times. You never forget your first partner, though, or how they died... especially how they died. Nothing can take away the feeling you get when it happens, the denial that strikes you in the moment; surreal, shocking, and all the other academic bullshit-terminology one can conjure up to describe what happens when your life changes in an instant. The cold steel of the barrel feels even colder when pressed against the roof of your mouth. But, hey, that's what whiskey was made for; to warm you up when you're so cold that your soul needs socks. And fuck, was I cold.

You never forget what it looks like, to stare into the eyes of someone as the life escapes their flesh. Cold. I could feel myself tightening the grip around the steering-wheel.

Smooth; that's how this car drives. It cuts through the smog of the night air, like a hot knife through margarine. An orange glow lit up my shades every now and again. The wind kept the cherry on my cig free of excess ashes. Crackling as I inhaled, the paper burned with an intensity that was now all but devoid in my life. I knew I was killing myself slowly, only because I was too much of a coward to kill myself in a quick manner. It was easier this way; to see myself slowly decay into my age. I should have just done it when I had the chance; when they took her from me. I was at rock bottom, it would have been easy. Unfortunately, Man is made to suffer, and good fuck, do I know about that. I reached for another cig, and turned the RadCom™ volume dial up; I love this beat. "J, you've got some great tunes..." "And you've got some pretty convincing artificial tits, Tracy. But I don't open my mouth to spoil the moment when I see 'em." "You're a fuckin' di-" I turned the music up louder, put a little more heft on the pedal, and drowned that whining circuit-job out with the roar of my V10.

"Alright," I stated, turning the music down, "We're almost there. 97, don't say a word, unless I speak to you, and not until after we're already inside. If you open your mouth, guaranteed our cover gets blown." He made a grimace and began to fidget. "Look, no offense, but you look and act like a fucking narc, so, just play it cool." 97 opened his mouth a bit, raised his hand with the index finger extended upwards as if he was going to say something profound; but he choked on his own thoughts, put his hand down, and just nodded in compliance. "Good lad. Now, Tracy, you're my arm candy until we get in;

then I want you to take the kid here, to the bar, and wait for me there. Yeah?" "Alright, Johnny, I can do that, but you know I'm on the clock, right?" she spouted from the rear. She better be cheap, or I'll just shoot her in an alley. I can't afford cat food *and* hookers this month.

We pulled into a ratty space under a Mega Pass. I was immediately accosted by the stench of piss, and damp mildew; seems about on par for this part of town. "*You aren't seriously parking me here, right? Look, I won't act up any more Johnny, please, come on...*" Automota chimed in as we came to a stop. "Well, I can't risk us being seen pulling up like the fucking circus just rolled in." "*Johnny, please, I'm beggin' ya sugar, some lunatic'll probably try to molest my tailpipe-*" "I'll put the top up and arm the anti-theft syst-" "*You fucking ass, I **am** the anti-theft system! And **I'm** telling you this is the sketchiest fucking place you've ever parked me! Even worse* *than that time when we went to Stank Nasty's® last mo-*" "Shut up, no one needs to hear about that. Just guard yourself, we won't be long." As I hopped out and started to look around, I could still hear Automota bitching behind me. The area was desolate; a concrete wasteland, filled with trash and painted in neon. Chainlink fences that were half torn apart stood as a mediocre deterrent against hoodlums gaining access to the underpass. Clearly, no city repair crews had been here in a long while. Puddles of oil-laden water gathered in the uneven pavement, giving off a luminescent glow in the dusky light. Cupping my hands around a fresh cigarette while lighting it, a cool breeze blew through the area. "Ew, is *that* dead?" squeaked Tracy, as she exited the car. She was clutching her bag and standing on one leg, pointing to a bundle of rags near a concrete support column. "*That*... is a homeless person, you fucking snob. And, there's a fifty percent chance that, yeah, he's fucking dead," I retorted, looking over my shoulder. Exhaling deeply, "You're a coin-slot prostitute, and you're telling me that you're programmed to still act like this? The absolute state of this world." I chuckled as I put my hands in my pockets and started down the street. "H-hey! W-wait up!" 97 scuffled along behind me, followed by the quick, clacking footsteps of Tracy's heels. Why me?

Ashes slowly fell from the end of my cigarette, drifting away in the foul wind of the city slums. To be fair, everything that was beneath the 40th story of the cityscape, was technically a slum. Bums sleeping in heaps of trash, marinating in their own waste; leaky pipes, flickering lights and signs; shady figures buying and selling who-knows-what in any shadow-clad nook and cranny they could fit themselves into: yeah, a veritable paradise of crime. Dingy, ramshackle merchant stalls lined the streets and alleys, peddling all sorts of horrid wares. "Hey, hey buddy," came a voice from one of the stalls we were passing on our way to the club. "Yeah, you, Mr. Fancy-Pants with the shades. Wanna buy some-" Without turning I spat, "Not interested 'bud.'" "Aw, come-on, you ain't gonna wanna miss this." Of course, Tracy had to be the one to get distracted by nonsense. "Alright, guy, what'cha sellin'?" she blurted out, coming to a complete stop and striking her programmed contrapposto pose. Several degenerates and vendors craned their necks this way and that, trying to get a better view of her shapely robo-ass. "Heheh, dose legs go all da-way up, sweetheart?" skeeved some passing urchin. "Beat it, punk, or I'll have your ass." I flashed my badge, which caused most of the alley-trash to go back to their business. 97 took the opportunity to explore a few stalls. The merchant Tracy was standing in front of almost lost a gallon of saliva from drooling. "Ain't nothin' I ain't got, hehe. But this, this here; it's somethin' special..." He reached behind his stall-counter and began fumbling with whatever it was he wanted to show her. "Look, man, we haven't got all day, and my patience is running fucking thin..." Irritated, I flicked my cigarette butt at him to hurry him up. "Yeah, yeah, pig, don't worry, your lady friend's got a right to see the merchandise-" "And I've got a right to shoot you without consequence, because rights don't exist; now hurry the fuck up." The merchant started to rummage more quickly. "Alright... take a look..." he pulled out a small folded cloth and shoved it in Tracy's direction. "What is it?" she asked softy, leaning over to get a better look. He began to unfold it, allowing for the street lights to hit whatever it was at just the right angle to cast a sparkle. "Ooooh..." Tracy's eyes got wide, and she leaned in closer. Had I not been watching, this would have been the end of her. All of a sudden, the merchant made a quick movement with his other hand towards Tracy's exposed neck- *BANG*

Tracy let out a quick scream and hit the deck like it was an air-raid. "AH FUCK!!" The merchant recoiled into his stall, knocking over several items on his way down. "Wh-what's happening?!" stammered 97, wheeling about to see what had happened. I stood there, pistol in-hand; smoke gracefully pouring from the barrel in the night air. "You picked the wrong Andro to harvest, asshole." I approached the stall. The merchant was writhing around amongst the items he had knocked over. He was clutching the hand I had shot, bleeding everywhere; making a scene. "N-no man, c'mon, I'm not that type-a' guy, man, I was just sellin' her some jewel-" "Yeah, sure, punk, and what's that then?" I motioned with my gun to a shattered device on the counter. He looked at it, then at me, then back at it, and again back to me. He looked deep into my eyes. I knew what was about to happen. "Don't try it; it'll be the end of you. Not that I care, but you might." Raising my pistol, I covered his cowering frame with the sights. "What happens next is on you..." He put both of his hands in the air, and choked up a bit. "You're lucky I'm in a rush, otherwise I'd book you right here and end your miserable ability to plague this already downtrodden place. People like you make me sick. I have half a mind to smoke you right now-" "No, man, please!" I thought he was going to piss himself. "Oh, so it's 'man' now, not 'pig.' Ha! How fast the winds of change blow through you when someone's got a gun. Get the fuck out of here, and if I see you again, I won't give you another chance. Yeah?" He nodded with such ferocity I thought his head would come off. Clutching his bleeding paw, he scrambled to his feet and fled like a crackhead looking for a rock. "Assclown," I muttered, holstering my gun. I lit another cig, and took a deep drag. Why the fuck does this seem to happen every day? "Tracy, are you paying rent down there? Get up, we've got shit to do." I started down the street again.

"Hey, Johnny..." came a faint, female voice from behind me. I didn't turn around, but I knew it was Tracy. "I, well, I just want to thank you for savin' my ass back there. Sorry about getting us into that mess. What was that thing anyway?" Exhaling, "It was a device that extracts the Neuro-Fluid© from Androids. That shit sells for top dollar on both the open and black markets. You're lucky, had he tapped you with it; there's no recovery from that. All of your data memory is in your Neuro-Fluid©, and even if you were to get away from him, and get it replaced, you wouldn't be the same person as you were. Not that you're a person anyway, but you get my drift." 97 decided to join the conversation, "B-but wh-what was he g-going to do after he g-got the Neuro juice? L-leave her s-standing there b-blank?" I took another deep drag, "If I hadn't been there? More than likely, he would have dragged her into his stall, to begin cutting her up for parts. But in this instance, he was probably going to do a quick extract, and run for it."

Tracy audibly shuddered at the concept. "Yeah, not a pretty thing. So stop fucking around." It wasn't far to the club now, probably another block, and it was nearing six PM. We were running low on time. If that Xio scum wasn't leaving early, we should catch him here. At the very least, I want to see who he's talking to. At best, I'd like to hold his grubby feet to the fire, and get some answers. And there it was, *Maze*™; an absolute hellhole for the degenerate underworld to fester and fuck in. Aside from the sign, it just appeared to be a large metal door in the side of a concrete complex. The building was clearly used for many purposes, including housing, but that's above street level.

They call it *Maze*™ for a reason; because it's a labyrinthine complex of underground venues for all sorts of debauchery. Finding your way around it took some getting used to; and no one should ever get used to such a place. I remember my first assignment that took me here, and I really wish I didn't. I really wish we weren't here now. But, hey, I have a job to do, even if it isn't official. I have a duty to make this city safer, regardless of how futile such a task was. I'd probably end up in some flooded gutter with a bullet in my back, and I was OK with that. Life is a ride, and I was about ready to jump off anyway. The heavy thumping from the club's bass-boosted music rattled my bones as we approached the entrance. A huge sign reading '*Maze*™' in pink neon hung over the doorway, illuminating the bouncer's shoulders. The glow framed his silhouette in pink, leaving only a void-black figure visible to us. Intimidating size; the guy had to be nearly two and a half metres tall. He was yoked like a cargo-bot. "Tracy, you're up."

"Hey there, big fella', mind letting me and my boy-toys in for a good time?" The bouncer leered over her to get a better look at me and the kid. In the deepest voice I've ever heard, "He's eighteen, right?" Tracy was a better actress than I anticipated. "He may not look it, bub, but that *man* packs it where it counts." She winked at the goliath and threw her hips to the side in a cocky, seductive manner. The big man looked over Tracy to eye up 97 again, then looked down at the Fembot. Without looking away from us, he reached backwards with one arm and knocked on the door. A peephole opened and I could see a glowing red orb look about. As quickly as it had opened, it shut again, and I could hear a large bolt sliding against rusty metal. The door slowly opened, blasting us with a stench of sex and deafening techno. Here we go.

"Thanks, sugar." Tracy led the way down the stairs into the red-light dungeon. The door must have been robotic; no one was on the other side of it. Only a stairwell leading down a flight of steps to a landing could be seen. The floor was covered with the grime of untold numbers of disgusting patrons, and who the fuck knows what else. All the lighting was red- mixed with black-light, giving everything an eerily dark-red tint with highlights. The three of us descended into the abyss of the city's bowels.

Chapter 8

Following Tracy's lead down the stairwell, we made our way down about five flights. We came to the final landing where an opening in the wall was concealed by a beaded drape. Pushing it aside, Tracy walked on through followed by 97, and myself in the rear. There was a large bar to our left with a few open stools. A few private booths lined the walls, all decently hidden from view with large velvet drapes. Needless to say, all the decor was red too, minus the protein stains on various surfaces revealed by the black-lights. Lovely. The orange glow from my cigarette illuminated my face and reflected off my shades. No one turned away from their drinks as we entered. I looked around for the entrance to the 'fun' rooms. To my right, past some booths, was another beaded-drape doorway. Another, in front of us past the bar, too. It might take me a bit to find this cretin, and time wasn't on my side. But, then again, nothing is ever on my side. "Tracy, take the kid to the bar, and grab a drink. I'm going to go find our friend."

She took 97 by the hand and led him to the bar, swaying her hips as she went. I swear the kid was sweating bullets; not because he was scared of the location, but because a girl just popped his hand-holding cherry. He's going to experience a lot of 'firsts' while hanging out with me.

As they sat down to order, I lit another cig with the butt of my last one. Alright, let's get on with this. Which door was that little bastard hiding behind? I didn't have much time and I didn't want to get lost down here and lose my opportunity to question him. Well, let's have a go at door number two; straight ahead, past the bar. I sauntered across the room towards the opposite side, passing Tracy and 97 at the bar. The floor was sticky, and I was just hoping it was spilled liquor. Approaching the bead-curtain, the music seemed to get louder; probably to drown out the screams of pain and ecstasy emanating from the depths of this place. You'd be surprised as to what money can buy in this city. Pushing the beads aside, I found myself in a long corridor with a number of doors on both sides; some shut, some open. The corridor led down to a T-junction, no doubt to more unfathomable shit. Slowly, I proceeded down the hallway, peeking into any room with an open door and listening as best I could outside the ones that were shut. Moaning, lots of moaning. The sound of flesh being punished by all manner of devices and tools could be heard echoing throughout the place. I peeked into a room about halfway down the corridor. *"Yes, yes! Oh, fuck yes baby, that's fuckin' it, right there!"* Nope.

Heavy, pulsating beats shook the walls around me. I peeked into another room towards the end of the hall. I barely stuck my head in. "Hey there, big boy! Come to get your anus wrecked, or just watchin'?" I couldn't believe my ears and eyes. A couple of naked midgets had a guy, also naked, tied to a bed on his stomach. Something was sticking out of his ass, and one midget was flogging him with a leather cat-o'-nine-tails. What the fuck. I had to ask, "No, I'm good. But you wouldn't happen to have seen a pudgy little Xio around, would ya?" The midget who wasn't engaged in flogging the naked patron stood for a second, scratching his dangling man-purse. Licking his fingers afterwards, he started talking with his mouth full. "Nah, haven't seen one, but, I've been in here ass-fuckin' this faggot for a couple hours, so I couldn't tell ya. Hehe, you sure you don't want in? He wouldn't know the difference of what went in there..." He kept licking his fingers as he began stroking himself with the other hand. I just turned and left. Some things should never be experienced.

Arriving at the T-junction, I paused. Right or left? This goon could be anywhere down here. I took a long drag and looked both ways. Last time I took a right turn, I ended up in a shoot-out, so, let's go left. Life is pretty raw when you have to make decisions based on the last time you almost died. But, such is life; my life, anyway. This hallway was lined with doors, too, no doubt hiding even worse perversions than the last corridor. I walked on, huffing my dart as I went. About halfway down, a faint noise penetrated one of the closed doors. It sounded like a phlegm-clogged, nasally voice. Leaning in, I got my ear as close to the door's surface as I was willing to get. "Oh, gawd! Yeah, dat's right, spank it, ooh, yeah!" That was definitely a Xio; but was it *my* Xio? Only one way to find out. Slowly opening the door, I peeked in. Inside was a female gimp, with a very wide black leather paddle that matched her latex gimp-suit. She was wailing away at the flabby ass of that same deck-captain I had been searching for. He was tied upside-down on an X-shaped crucifix facing away from the door towards the back wall. Sitting in a chair in the corner to my right laid all of his clothes, including his stupid little hat. Sneaking in, I shut the door behind me.

Smack, Smack, Smack; I leaned against the wall, closest to the door next to the chair with all the Xio's things. So, this is what he spent his money on when he wasn't being a shady business-man. Ha, like I can even call him a 'man' after seeing this. About five minutes passed; so, I lit up another cig as I waited for the gimp to finish tanning his hide. The flick of the lighter flint went unnoticed against the backdrop of heavy techno and the sound of leather clapping flesh. I had time to wait; it wasn't like he was going anywhere without me knowing it. Glancing down at the chair, I noticed that there were some unusual bulges in his suit jacket. Probably some documents; what luck. If this guy was a one-stop-shop to solving this thing, I'd be elated. *Smack, Smack, Smack*. I wonder how Tracy and 97 were getting on? Hopefully she didn't let him get drunk, that would be a nightmare to deal with, I'm sure. I say that, like I'm not in a dungeon of nightmares as-is. The sounds of spanking ceased, and I looked up to see what had caused the lack of commotion. The gimpess put her paddle down to her side, seemingly taking a break. She turned, and slightly jumped at the sight of me. Her eyes got noticeably wider as she looked through her zipper-slits. Up and down she looked over me in a studious way. One foot in front of the other in choreographed fashion, she walked over to me. Placing her gloved, left hand up to her mouth – *zzziipp* – she opened the zipper-slit covering her talk-hole. A soft, almost whimsical voice greeted me. "Mind if I bum one?" Not what I was expecting, but alright, we'll see how this plays out. I reached into the inside pocket of my jacket, and pulled out my pack of Outer Rims™. Holding the pack out, she removed her right glove to reveal a porcelain-white hand. Her fingernails were painted a vibrant red. Surprisingly elegant; but I'm not sure what I was expecting. Outstretching the delicate, almost frail hand, she daintily plucked a cigarette from the pack. "Thanks. Mind if a girl gets a light?" I obliged and produced my lighter; - *flick* - the flame ignited the end, producing a cherry that burned a hot orange, nicely accenting those ruby-red nails. As she leaned in a bit closer, to get the cig-end good and toasted, I noticed her lips were the same shade of red as her nails, and her eyes were a pleasant green; almost emerald. Oddly enough, she was seemingly pretty, despite the fact I had to look through a layer of zippers and latex to admire any bit of her. "So, what's your safeword?" she exhaled, looking me up and down. "Give me ten minutes." Flashing my badge, I motioned with my thumb towards the door. "Alright, I could use a drink anyhow. See ya in ten, stud." She opened the door and slinked out.

"Is dat yous, Taz, I t'ought I heard someone else come in. Ya gonna give me da numba'? Hehe…" "You fucking wish, sicko." I walked over to the chair and picked up his stuff, rummaging to see what I could find. "Wh-who's dare? I got powerful friends, you'll regre-" "Yeah, yeah, shut the fuck up." Reaching into his coat pockets, I felt an envelope. Bingo. Examining it, I saw that it was a blank manila envelope with a fat stack of papers enclosed. Opening it, I checked the front page: *Protocols of the Shareholders of Xiotron©®™SM*. Well, that's interesting, but not what I'm here for. For now, I needed answers, and I wasn't about to read some corporate dissertation to obtain them; who had time for that? Sealing the envelope back up, I tossed it down near the door. Ah, his wallet; *Yariel Seinman, 57, 65-67-68…* "Interesting digits, Yari. Almost like they were chosen, not generated. How high up do you go for that kind of privilege?" Tossing the wallet to the ground with the coat, I knocked the rest of his filthy shit to the floor; picked the chair up, and moved it closer to the sexually arrested Xio. Planting the chair backwards behind him, I took a seat, using the back as an arm rest. "Okay, Mr. Seinman, now, you're going to tell me what was in that crate I signed for the other day, yeah?" "Oh... gawd, fuck..." "Is that a *yes*, or do I need to get physical?" I exhaled in his direction. "C-come-on man, I'm just da guy who does da shippin', I don't got no clue what yer tawkin' 'bout, honest!" "An honest Xio; now that's a new one." He let out an ear piercing howl as I burned his blubbery ass with my cigarette. "You can scream as loud as you want, no one will care down here, bud. I can keep this up for a long time; I've got a whole pack to burn through. And seriously, I love to smoke, so you're in for a rough ride." Quite possibly, I chose the wrong wording considering this tubby twink probably gets ridden pretty rough. I shuddered in disgust at my own thought.

"What was in the fucking crates?!" I was getting agitated at his lack of immediate cooperation. "I ain't tawkin', you ain't got enough money t' convince me, an' ya ain't got da stones t' get it outta me-" "Oh, is that the case, then? Suit yourself." Standing up, I shifted to the left, grabbed the chair, and lifted it into the air. "Last chance." "Fuck you, pig." "Wrong answer." Plastic splinters and chair legs went flying in all directions as I shattered the seat across his wide back. "JESUS FUCK, AHHH!!" Blood droplets began to form on the striations where the sharp parts of the ruined chair lacerated him. "Ok, look, I-" "And I don't give a fuck, you had your chance. Now I'll have some fun before I ask you another question." "P-please..." "Well, at least you're asking nicely for this beating." Cocking my leg back, I drove my boot-toe into the back of his dangling skull with dreadful force. The *thud* was satisfying, but I hope I didn't kill him; I need some info first. "You still alive, you bitch?" "Uhhhh..." "Good enough."

I gave his ribs a solid right hook. Then a left. Another right. Like a boxer in one of those ancient 20th Century flicks wailing away on a butchered side of beef. I was tenderizing him real nice like. Hell, I might even cut me off a slice and take it home to kitty. Taking a step back to admire the carnage, "You ever piss blood?" -*flick*- Exhaling, I started shaking my fists out; get a little loose for round two. "Uhhhh..." "Yeah, and you aren't gonna shit right for a while either." I dove right back in like a fucking ringside champ.

"Alright, Piggy, let's play 'Seinman Says.' Sound fun?" Shaking from the muscle convulsions and pain, he began to moan, "P-please..." "Seinman Says: tell the nice man what the cargo consisted of." I bent down a bit to hear a little more clearly. "It's c-c-classified company property, I'm n-not aut'ori-" "Yeah, sure." Standing up, I drove my knee into his back with all my might. His mouth flew open wide like his eyes. The most faint of screams; as the air was knocked from his lungs. "I'll start cutting body parts off, Seinman, don't doubt me." "S-s-stopp!!" "Then fucking talk, you stubborn bastard!" With difficult breathing, he spat, "Y-you're lives... are w-wort'less... heh..." Cracking my knuckles, "You'll learn..." I wonder what will give out first; my fists, or his fat? Let's see.

"How's that spine?" "Uhh, huh, p-p-plleeaaaassseee!!!!" Stepping off to the side, I knelt down close enough to his face that I could hear him without being in biting distance; you just can't be too careful. "Okay, Piggy, squeal for me." He started coughing a bit, expelling flecks of crimson with every desperate breath. In a hushed whisper, he gargled, "D-da c-c-caargo is c-c-lassif-" "So your life is a joke to you?" Grabbing him by his twisted, black hair, I yanked his head down to my level. "You're going to talk, or I'm going to get a bit more feral, yeah?"

His nasty little eyes slowly rolled over to look me in the face. "F-f-fuc-" "Oh-ho-ho, my god! You just want," I stood up in a millisecond, "to die today; do you fucking not?" Again, I kneed him hard in his scoliosis-plagued spine; like that Belgian Kung-Fu guy. This time, I threw in some kicks, to complement my ruthless fists. His body became quickly bruised and his gurgling and coughing only became less frequent. *-flick-* Taking a long drag, I leaned against the wall to my left near the fat man's crucifix. The sound of a man urinating on himself, isn't something you tend to forget; I'm sure he shaved today, so that probably stings a bit.

A stench wafted up from the dark-yellow-reddish puddle of piss gathering beneath the Xio's head. "Pissing blood ain't fun, bud, I suggest you talk." Just then, the door creaked open. My eyes darted over to see the gimptress slowly creeping back in. In her left hand, she was holding a pinkish cocktail in a martini glass; which had, floating within, a little olive skewered on a green plastic sword. Cute. "Ooh, don't mind me-" She closed the door behind her. "-I won't get in the way of a good time." She made an over-dramatic wink, bending over and saluting with her right hand. This woman *has* to be human. Her paddle was tied to her leather belt; sitting just right at her latex-clutched waist. Exhaling, "Mind if I borrow that?" Reaching out to make a grabbing gesture, I stopped at the sound of the Xio making some attempt to speak. "K-Kit... Kits... guhg..." He started coughing up blood. "Don't you die on me, you little fucker!!" I dove down to just outside the pool of urine; I needed to hear this. "Kits... *K*-Kitss in... da c-c...c..raatehhuu..." His breathing ceased. "Fuck!"

God dammit. What did that mean? 'Kits in the crate?' Kits of what? Or, for what? To build what? What was Xiotron©®™℠ building? Whatever it was, the terrorists seemingly wanted it, or wanted to destroy it. Or prevent it? There were too many questions, and I needed answers. "Hey, uh, is he gonna be okay?" She took a sip from the glass; her lip-zipper clanking on the rim. I stood up and began heading for the door. Stopping when I got to the gimpette, "You got a scanner on you?" She produced a small, square cube; no bigger than a gambling die. Its surface was transparent, revealing all the circuitry within. I reached for my PFC© (Personal Finance Card©,) waved it over the cube, and let the IR-reader do its thing. "Charge the account for the inconvenience." Going again for the door, "And, toots," turning my head to look at her before the door shut, "sorry about the mess."

Chapter 9

It was extremely difficult for me to wrap my mind around what was happening. I felt like I was getting myself into a completely different life. Terrorists, major Corps, espionage; who was I anymore? Just last week I was worried about finding missing kids; now I've been shot at in a fucking warzone, and I just beat a man to death in a nightclub. My life was really falling apart fast. And now it was only a matter of time before this whole thing blows up on me. I needed to think of a plan ASAP. How was Curden involved? Was he just the lackey? How much did he know? Did he know anything at all? The only real way to find out, is if I take him up on his offer. I'd have to pretend to be corrupt and power hungry enough to want to work for him off the books. So be it.

Emerging from the beaded doorway, I rejoined the gang in the barroom. Tracy turned to me as I approached. Her artificial eyes glowed with a white ring around the iris; a pretty neat effect caused by the black-lights. "Holy shit, what happ-" "Don't ask questions, Tracy. Let's go, I'll explain later." She must have noticed what I neglected to: my hands were bruised and bloody. "D-d-did you find h-hi-" "What part of 'shut the fuck up and get your shit in gear' do you not get?" "R-right." Both paid their tabs and got up to follow me out. I didn't look at anyone on the way out. Couldn't risk anyone remembering my face. To be fair, though, what are they going to describe? A white guy in shades, smoking a cig? Dime-a-dozen. I was probably more paranoid than I needed to be, as I'm sure that wasn't the first guy to die down here tonight, nor would he be the last. I'm sure they've got privacy policies and insurance, so as long as that span-dame keeps her mouth zipped, I should be good. What a club.

The large iron door opened, expelling us onto the streets from the bowels of the underworld. I began to walk fast towards where we parked. "Hey, Johnny, what fucking happened back there?" She had a right to know, but I didn't know how to explain it quite yet. "Wait till we get to the car." I fumbled for another cigarette. It didn't take long for us to get back to the ride. "*I swear to my circruitry, Johnny, you leave me in another fucking place like this, I'm gon-*" "Automota, we need to leave and I have no time for this." "*Oh. Okay, I'll set the GPS; where to?*" I paused for a second as I made myself comfortable in the driver's-seat, "District 21. The precinct." As the roof retracted, 97 got in the passenger side and looked at me wide-eyed. The heavy *thud* of Tracy's mechanical ass hitting the back seat let me know I could hit the gas. "You know, Johnny, I said it before, but I think now is a good time to remind you that-" "Yeah, yeah, you aren't free, I get it. Just figure out a price and I'll pay it... I don't even know if I'll be alive much longer to care." I muttered that last bit. "'Kay, J-man, whatever you say." -*pop*- went the sucker-pop she was tonguing while reclining and kicking her feet over the side of the car.

The roar of the engine echoed along the concrete highways. 97 started staring at me again. "S-so? What h-happened?" "I killed him." All at once, Tracy, 97, and Automota exclaimed, "*You what?!*" -*flick*- "Yeah, I fucking killed him. I didn't intend to, but that's what happened. What matters is that Xiotron©®™℠ is up to something and seemingly everyone is involved, including these terrorists, somehow. I want to know what's going on. The Xio said that there were kits of some kind in the crates. So, something is being built off-world that no one is supposed to know about. And that's why they needed us, a corporate entity with inspection authority. They couldn't *legally* do it without a signature, but they also couldn't compromise the operation by having expendables, like us, figure out what was going on. We might spill the soup on the whole outfit, and that would lead to-" 97 interjected, "Terrorists! I-if people knew wh-what they were u-up to, they w-would tell the t-t-terrorists. Wait, are th-they actually th-the bad guys? Wh-what side are w-we o-on?" The kid had a good point. As far as I could tell, we were getting shot at from all sides. We were on our own in this. "Listen, 97, I can't ask you to help me in what I'm thinking of doing. So, I'm going to drop you off back at my place before I head to the precinct. If you could do me a favour and walk Tracy back home, that would be real nice of you." Tracy just had to start talking, "Wow, J-bird, that's pretty sweet of ya. I guess killin' that guy really flipped your switch, huh?" "I don't have a lot of money, Tracy, don't make me get greedy. I'm not above murder, clearly." 97 was twirling his thumbs about, looking out over the city-scape as we drove on. "Y-you know, I n-n-never had any f-friends, and I d-don't think th-that'll change anytime s-s-soon.

I'd r-rather d-die in one g-good-d adventure, th-than r-r-rot at the o-office." A smile crept across my jaded face. "Alright then, partner, let's catch us some bad-guys."

"Uh, hey, '*heroes*?' Yeah, I'm still back here! I really hope you don't think I'm tryin' to accompany you ass-monkeys on some crazy quest." I exhaled into the night sky, "Tracy, what have you ever done with your life that was worth a damn?" "I'm programmed to be a whore, asshole!" "Well, wanna fix that?" She sat up and leaned over my shoulder, putting her weight on the seat and centre armrest, "What do you mean?" "I mean, do you want to override your programming?" "Johnny, that's illegal as fuck. How would you even pull that off?" I elbowed Tracy off the centre armrest and opened the compartment it concealed. Fumbling around for a moment, I held up a small data chip. "This, this is your key to freedom, Tracy." Shutting the compartment with my arm,

I inserted the chip into Automota's micro-drive.

"*Oooh, yeahhh. Illegality tastes so, mmm, gooood.*"

"Th-that's wh-why your c-car is so w-weird! Y-you h-h-hacked it!" blurted 97, flailing his arms about like a lunatic. "Here's the deal, I can unlock your systems and remove all the stop-thoughts and fail-safes; but I want something in return." "Uh-uh, that'll cost you, I don't do that shit for free..." I craned my neck around to glance at her. "I'm talking about helping me out with this crime issue. If anyone needs some of your *talents*, it'll be Mr. Floppy over here." "Wh-what's th-that mean?" "Shut up. Now, Tracy, what'll it be?" She sat deep back into the rear bench-seat. Her arms were crossed, and she was looking this way and that. I could tell her wires were firing, and she was struggling against her own programs. "Y-yes? Sure, why not." "How did you override that?" "I logged it under an unknown update. Whatever happens isn't my fault in the equation." "Crafty. Anyway, plug in to Automota; there's a jack in the back, should be in the centre there behind the armrest." She looked around for a moment, then found the cord. Plugging it into her right ear-hole, she sat perfectly still, hands in her lap.

"Alright, run the reboot." "*Sit tight, hun, this won't take but a moment...*" In the rearview mirror, I could see Tracy go stiff as a board. Her eyes widened fully, and she developed a slight twitch in the corner of her upper lip. "She'll be like that for a moment, so let's go over my plan." 97 nodded in agreement. "So, Curden told me that I didn't have what it takes to play ball, that I wouldn't go corrupt for money. He's right, so I'll pretend like I will for another shady job. Hopefully he doesn't catch on. My plan is to get another crate location from Curden, get there early, and set a trap. We bust the guys with the crate, and finally see what's inside. If we're lucky, the terrorists won't attack this time and we can get to the bottom of this. Sound good?" "I-I'm not r-really a good sh-shot, you know?" "Top in your class? Stop being modest; it looks bad on you." I laid on the gas a little heavier. "Automota, phone Curden." Hopefully he's at the office. He probably was, simply because he couldn't take his dope-chair with him, and I don't know what he'd do without his Phyx©. The centre console displayed the little ringing icon for about a minute before, "Hello? Who's callin'?" The little icon changed to a smiley-face, indicating I was connected. Ironic, because I know that joker wasn't smiling on the other line; and neither was I. "Milton, It's John. I want to take you up on that offer, you know, that job you said I was too chicken-shit to take. I want in." There was silence for a moment, plagued only by Curden's disgusting breathing. "Johnny, Johnny boy, J-mac-daddy..." How fucked up on this stuff was he? "Hehe, alright, you prick, I knew you'd come around. I may have a job for ya. Where are you currently?" "I'm actually on my way to the office, I'll be there in twenty minutes." "That's good news, Johnny, hehe, fuckin', yeah, you two bit fuckin'-" -*click*- He hung up. All I was left looking at, was the BellEnd Telecom™ logo, telling me I owed nine-fifty in fees. I need a new provider; *Jog*Mobyl® supposedly fixed their 20G coverage and the towers don't give off radiation anymore. People are still going sterile from the telecom systems being installed, but you do get free calls, both Lunar and Terrestrial. Things to consider.

Chapter 10

We pulled up to the imposing Precinct building. Parking in a small lot out-front, I addressed my robotic companions. "Alright, we're going in to get the info, then we'll be back out. We'll make a plan then." I realized Tracy was still zoned out. "Shit. Okay, 97, you have to stay here with her and keep an eye on the car. Yeah?" He nodded, and began looking about from his seat. "And, Automota, make sure he doesn't get any funny ideas while tin-tits is passed out in the back, get me?" *"Don't worry, Johnny, he has to watch out for himself when I'm around... rraawrr..."* God dammit.

Strolling up the wide marble stairs leading to the precinct's entrance, I took one last long drag from my cig. "Here we go," I muttered, flicking the spent butt to the side. The large glass doors opened by motion-sensor, beckoning me into the sun-bright lobby. Barely crossing the threshold, I was greeted by a familiar chime.

"*Special Jurisdictions Unit 88, Agent, Peiler, Johnathan; what a pleasure to see you tonight. Is there anything I can prepare for you while you are en route to your destination?*" "Not today, Penny. I'm just going to see Curden." I approached the elevator, but it didn't open for some reason. "Penny, what gives?" "*Mr. Curden is in a meeting currently, Agent Peiler. You will kindly wait in the lobby until his meeting is concluded.*" A yellow light began to flash, grabbing my attention. From the floor to the left of the elevator had emerged a white, stool-shaped pylon. Apparently, I'm supposed to wait here. Sitting down, I began to think over everything that had happened in the past few days. I couldn't help but think that the guy that shot at me on my way to work was somehow hired to kill me. Was I on to something? Before this whole thing started, I was on the trail of kidnappers, not illegal parts-shipping. What would have been the angle if he was a hired gun? It just doesn't add up. None of this adds up.

There had to be some piece to the puzzle I was overlooking, something that I missed. The info Penny sent to Automota a few days ago, revealed only that there were no seeming connections to any of the missing children. They came from all different districts, different economic classes. There were, however, more females on the list of abductees than there were males; but that's always the case. There was a two percent higher number of abductees from district 20A but there were also more children there. Higher crime, too. Two percent was within the margin of error, but it still didn't sit right with me. Other than that, nothing was particularly unique about any of the cases. To be fair, not a single body was ever recovered. We had no leads. We didn't have anything. What did concern me, however, was that the last two agents that were working on those cases also disappeared. But, it was on a mission that was completely unrelated if I recall correctly. In fact, that might be something I need to look into.

"Penny, send all data on the disappearances of agents 45 and 201 to my personal drives, and forward them to my car." *I have forwarded all information on ** Case 395-047B: Concerning the disappearance of Agent Hal van Dreer, Badge 45 – and Agent Yoshihiru Amasaka, Badge 201 ** to your personal systems. Is there something else I can do for you while you wait, agent?* "I don't think so, no." *You are welcome, agent Peiler.* Fucking passive-aggressive AI. ** *Bing Bong* ** You'd think, with all this tech, they would have upgraded those stupid alert sounds.

Stepping into the lift, I went to lean against the back wall. The doors made a little *click* and *hiss* sound, as they closed. You never seem to be amazed or taken-aback when you notice something fresh about a thing you've seen a thousand times. I needed to think about what exactly I was going to tell Curden. He would, most probably, get wise to my lying if I fucked this up, so I needed to be on my best game if I wanted to pull this off. What do I even say? Honestly, I should just let him do the talking, maybe he thinks I'm too stupid to understand the intricacies of all of this. And that, that angle there, is how I'll stay ahead of him. If he thinks I'm too stupid to understand anything, he may not think about everything he says. Or, he may not think that I'm planning anything, and just give me the assignment without question. Why do I even make up scenarios in my head? I guess I would just have to act normal and see what happens.

'You have arrived at the
Eighty-third
floor. Please exist with care!'

This view will never get old. No matter how much I hate this city and all the shitty inhabitants, I'll always admit: That it's one gorgeous sea of neon.

It came complete with the rolling waves of uncountable tenement buildings and shopping megaliths. Crashing and breaking upon each other; culminating in enormous, jutting spires of iron and light. There was never one building tallest among the others; always some rival upon the next outcrop or across the bay, to another horizon of light-pollution in the night. One could almost get sucked in to simply watching the city crawl beneath them, never to wake from the trance. I wonder if that's why Milton never seems to go home? "Heh..." Audibly chuckling to myself, I proceeded left, towards the cluster of egg-chairs at the far point of the oddly shaped, ovular office space. The chairs were all arranged in the same fashion as before, but Curden was facing towards the window; I couldn't see anything except his spindly legs, dangling over the side of his chair. Barely making it to the edge of the seating assortment, a voice. "I can smell you, John." I froze. That was possibly the weirdest shit that has ever been said to me, and I have no idea if he's serious. "Heh, heh, yeessss. Yes, John, Johnny Rockets, Jizzle Johnson, Oh, yes…" I could hear him take a deep, wheezy breath. "Yes, I can smell your wretched hide from here. You reek of…" His chair whipped about with such speed, I was taken by utter surprise. "…of **bitch**! HA, HA, HA! That's what! You smell of bitch! And I know a bitch when I smell one! You came crawling in here like you wanted a piece of the pie; but honestly, Johnny, I don't think you have what it takes to hack it in this industry. What are you after? Money? Stock options? Women; nah, course not, haha. You couldn't betray your dear…" "I'll shoot your withered ass right here, Milt," I interjected, standing a bit forward. I swear on my life, if he says some off-kilter shit… "No, no, Johnny, no, you dumb bitch, you can't be bought out so easily. So? What, then, is it? What, do you possibly want out of this engagement?" Curden rested his elbows on his knees and, almost by instinct, interlocked his fingers, resting his pointy, icicle-looking chin on the finger cradle he made for himself. Before I could get a word out of my half-cracked mouth, "No, please, have a seat, *partner*. I wouldn't want such a bold man to go standing now, after all, you're a prominent man now, a real..." His slimy, putrid tongue slithered out from behind his fragmented enamel spears; slowly lubricating his puckering speak-hole, "...*criminal*."

There's no way Curden knows about what happened at the club tonight. There's simply no fucking way. He has to be referring to something else. Alright; play dumb. I took my seat as calmly as possible. "I have no idea what you're talking about." Really? That's what I came up with? Whatever joy there might have seemingly been in Milton's eyes rapidly faded. "I'm talking about the fucking fact that your retarded ass got a taste of some action and wants more. Well, here's the skinny; you work for me now. Don't worry about another terrorist attack;

we're pretty sure we've got that under control. You've got a job in two days, same as before: sign for the goods, no questions. This one pays. Two hundred thousand credits. No transfer; I've got it on a physical drive." He produced a small metallic rectangle, about two and a half centimetres thick, by five centimetres wide and ten centimetres long; and slapped it onto the table. Now, I didn't notice this table rise from the centre of the floor space, but it had suddenly become part of the decor. It, too, was clad in white plastic, as if the objects in the building could simply manifest as needed out of this malleable, plastic coating. Though, it was still hard as steel. But, now is no time to get distracted by furniture. Two hundred grand was a lot of money, even with the hyper-inflation factored in. A guy could get rich through corruption. But, now I was at a junction: do I abandon my compatriots, lead them to their doom, possibly arrest them, and take the money? Should I make this the new chapter of my life story? I could do a lot with a steady stream of money like this. I could also continue with my plan and bust this whole thing, and fight, and most probably die, for something as intangible as 'morality.' I don't think I'm being given enough time to think about this, given the gravity of the situation.

I've always had to be out for myself, and this could be a big break. I never got anything in my life that I didn't have to fight for. And honestly, who was I kidding? This city would never be free from the ever-increasing crime. The only thing I could do was adapt and evolve. I had to be worse than the world around me. "Alright, but I'll prove you wrong, Milt. I want double." Curden's eyes got wide for a moment, only to narrow as his grin became wide instead. "So, every man has a price, yeah? Heh, heh..." he sleazed, fishing about in his trouser pocket for another small, metallic brick. "Ah!" he exclaimed, placing the second credit-block ever so daintily on top of the first. He sat back in his chair, so smug, and pleased with himself;

as if he had just convinced Eve to eat the apple. "Go on, take it. Who do you have in your miserable life that would even give a fuck if you turned up dead in a gutter tomorrow? Who are you trying to impress with your false sense of morality? Go on, taste it. Revel in it. Stain yourself with this," he inhaled deep. Exhaling with a twisted grin, "...*sin*. You're like a lamb, J-Man. Except, you were stained long before I found your worthless carcass on my fucking employment roster! Haha. And, no one minds losing a stained lamb, Johnny." This sadist was privately getting off to our involvement in some criminal, black-market scandal. I can see why he chose 97; only someone so weak willed could be coerced into this shit. But, I could now really understand why he hated me; I never caved to him in the past. He must be ecstatic.

My fingertips grazed the surface of the credit-blocks. "With this contract, I own you. Our covenant, Johnny, our sacred bond. You take this golden calf, and *thine soul art mine*." He leaned in over towards me, palms down on the table, straddling my arm and the money. By the time I realised how bloodshot his abyssal eyes were, he was crawling on all fours upon the table. He was as close to me as he could be without actually touching me. I felt him exhaling on my face with his foul, noxious breath. I could smell his rotting insides as if they were exposed to me in plain view. His skin was cracked, dry, flaking off as he moved; as if he was decomposing by the moment. A hissing whisper broke the silence, "I can smell you, John. I can smell your soul, and it is rife with malice and hate." Curden's eyes became wide, and they rolled into the back of his skull. He recoiled swiftly, but not in haste; finding himself curled up in his chair. I took the money from the table and put the bricks in my coat pocket.

"Mr. Curden, your scheduled dose of Phyx© is due to commence. Please sit up straight." Struggling with great effort, Milton pulled himself to an upright position.

-tsssk-

"They've got you on a schedule, now, aye, Milt?" "S-shut up, Johnny. You don't get it, you don't get how it helps me think. I know things, now, that I never could have before. I'm smarter, Johnny. I read this book – you've probably never heard about it – called, *Holy Bible*. Have you read it?" "I've read a couple chapters, interesting characters. It's the only real book I own." I didn't have a good answer. "Oh, so maybe you aren't a fucking retard after all, huh, Johnny?" "You really gotta lay off that juice, Milt, it's enslaving your mind." His eyes darted up towards me; teeth bared, he snapped, "And what do you know of servitude?! I serve a higher purpose, J-man! I know how to talk to God! To God, Johnathan!

To *fucking* God! You read the book, you gain the knowledge – I am as the machine my Creator has programmed me to be! One with the collective. You filthy troglodyte! You hide away and reject your rightful place in servitude! Apostate! What know you of Salvation?!" Hissing, he curled up into his egg-chair; like some feral fetus in a plastic womb. What the fuck is happening to him?

-tsssk -

Frozen by disbelief, I waited until Milton unruffled his feathers. He slowly calmed down, and came to a normal sitting position. His eyes took a moment to stop twitching this way and that. With a shaky, skeletal hand, he wiped the froth from the corners of his quivering lips. Cracking his neck in a very slow, deliberate manner, - *pop* - "Aahh, you know, J-daddy, heh, heh, you know? You know? So; you, you take the money. Okay, great. He takes the

162

money..." I was pretty sure Curden was just talking to himself at this point. I thought I'd take the opportunity to ask this junkie some questions he might not normally be inclined to answer. "Yes, I took the money, thank you. So, Mr. Curden, how are shares in Viizor™ looking these days?" Reclining in my egg-chair, I took a second to enjoy a taste of corruption. The seat wasn't actually that bad; it wasn't as good as my chair back home, but hey, not everything can be *that* chair. Never once did I stop to examine my surroundings in any great detail in this office. This chair's interior was lined with a fine, white plush that glistened in the soft, pearlescent light emanating from the room's edges. It looked like snow but felt like a cloud. I'm also assuming that hidden in this little shell are all kinds of gadgets to listen to or record me. And, likewise, I'm sure I had a Phyx© injector poised at the ready to dose me up.

Curden sleazed his way back into a slouching position, resting his elbows upon his knees again. "If you're looking at investing corporately with your earnings, let me tell you that Viizor™ is about to go through the roof. And I mean soon, Johnny, real soon. Phyx© is about to go public, and they are just readying the last of the first shipments; destination, Earth. The colonies will get theirs later, but the company is looking to be able to service almost eighty-percent of the terrestrial market within half a year of launch. This is going to be huge, J Master Flex, – yeah, you, that's right, big man on the block – you could get rich, my man. Invest even half of that in Viizor™, and you'll be rich beyond your wildest dreams, Johnny." I had to pause and think for a moment. A person has to have access to a broker to get into the stock trade, and those aren't cheap these days. "Alright, Milt, say I want to invest? How do I get the money to a broker? What's the charge, et cetera?" Wheezing as he inhaled deeply, "You just leave that to me, Johnny boy. I happen to know a broker. I'll give you his card; just make sure you play ball, yeah?" I stared into the voids of pitch, nestled deep in the sunken sockets of his narrow skull. "Yeah."

Light, when penetrating smoke, has a dazzling effect. Colours; dancing in the night sky, like so many dreams – pretty, and always out of reach. And once, if you could, by some luck, you grabbed one: your hand goes right through it. Moral of the story: your dreams aren't tangible, and the only way to ever obtain them is to build them. Unfortunately for me, I didn't have dreams; just the smokes to create the image for people to ruminate on. This money was real enough, and I had a few plans of my own to attend to. I think I was finally getting the hang of this world. Scary, sure, but I had a feeling that there was someway to really make a dent in some fiend's pocket-book.

Popping my collar up around my face, I descended the flowing marble stonework. Unintentionally or not, I took my time getting back to the car. I really had a lot to think about. What was I supposed to do? Keep playing the game; or bust this thing as soon as I unearth evidence at this new job? The money is nice, but so is justice. It's a 'crossed circuit' for sure. To be fair, there isn't much justice in this nightmare-realm, so it's safe to say I don't make a difference. But, on the contrary, there are those few; those desperate few, trying so hard to fight against this rampant injustice – that they may be inspired by my sacrifice. Or, I'm being a fucking moron and need to get some sleep.

"97," the car door opened heavily, and I climbed in, "I want you to go into the office on whatever days you are scheduled to go in. Business as usual, yeah? Until I call you for the next job. It'll be a few days, so you can get some R&R." - *flick* –

Exhaling, "Automota, what's the status of Tracy?" Looking back to the rear seat, I didn't have to wait for the car's assessment of the situation; she was still stiff, eye-lids and lips twitching. "*She's at ninety-two percent, Baby, heh, heh, yeaaahh. Freedom's pretty sweet, honey, you'll love it...*" "We can do without the theatrics, *honey.*" "*I wasn't even addressing that last bit to you, fucker.*" "Like I give a damn-" "*You'll give a damn plus more when I fucking run us into a lamp-post you worthless fa-!*" "L-l-listen! Y-you two sh-sh-shut up!" 97 hastily interjected. "Anyway, come over in two days; we'll talk about a plan then." Roaring into the night, we sped off down the highway.

Chapter 11

All that could be heard above the dead silence, was the sound of ice cracking as room-temperature liquor was poured over it. I'd take Curden's advice and invest half, two-hundred thousand, in corporate shares. We'll see how this gambit pays off. I hadn't blown the rest of the loot either; I set aside a bit for 97. After all, he deserved something. I bought myself some goodies, that's for sure. And probably too much of this Cognac. I wasn't a glutton though, and I was trying to cut back on smoking a tad – I was on the same pack since I took my motley-crew to the club; probably a new record for me. To be fair, I was down to three cigs, and I had them rationed. I was certainly going to need one after 97 comes by, and then leaves, when I brief him tonight. The next two, I'll try to make last through until lunch tomorrow. Luckily, I have a backup pack for when I run out. And I know I'll run out. The reports on van Dreer and Amasaka were almost entirely classified. Not a bit of useful info on them, not even who issued their orders, nothing.

Something wasn't right, and I could feel I was in for a rough experience. I know this isn't going to be pretty, and nothing is really going to get me ready for it. 97 will most likely piss himself and run. I don't think I could blame him. Well, better get this over with.

Picking up the phone, I was accosted by that glitchy hag; the operator drone. "*How may I, may I, may I help you, Sir?, Sir?, Sir?*" My face was on the verge of erupting with lava-hot blood, "Call Harold Flynn, Agent 97, GDC." My fingers made a constant drumming, as I tapped them in frustration upon my desk. "*Calling H-H-H-Harold Flynn, have a, a, a, a nice day!, a nice day!, a nice day!*" I leaned my head far back in my chair and tapped my forehead with the barrel of my pistol. God dammit, I'd do it right now, you stupid fucking machine, you have no idea... "He-hello? Wh-who's calling?" The weak voice confirmed it was my guy. "97, hey, it's 88, it's time. Come to my place in a couple hours, and we'll talk then."

"Y-yeah, n-n-no p-problem-m." *click* – Did I have time for another drink?

The answer was 'yes,' and it was 'yes' for the next three. There's a point where a man stops giving a shit. Plus, I wasn't driving anywhere tonight; definitely not now. Almost exactly two hours after 97 hung up on me, a soft, feminine knocking graced my door. There, in the peep-hole again, was that greasy geek; 97. Creaking on its metal hinges, the door slowly opened. I looked down at the kid and he stared back at me through those telescopic lenses; his eyes, magnified to such an extreme, it caused discontent. "You're never going to procreate looking like that. You know that?" "W-w-wow! Th-that's what y-you called m-me over f-for?!" "No, but I'll take the moment to give you some unsolicited advice. You look like a complete skeeze; like you write programs to sexually satisfy other sad men's AI bang-bots." His mouth was agape, body hunched over as if he was just punched in the gut. He looked down at himself, then back up at me. "Th-this is a new c-c-coat, a-ass-w-wipe." He made a jerking motion to his grotesque see-through sport-coat. Since when did he get so defensive? Stepping back into the room, I motioned with my head for 97 to come in. He proceeded to scuffle inside and I shut the heaving door behind him – taking one last good look, just to make sure he wasn't tailed.

Taking my seat again after shuffling past my guest, I lit a cig out of habit. Oh, well. Exhaling with the cigarette hanging from my lips, "You want a drink?" I poured myself a glass, and hovered the mouth of the bottle over a second empty glass. Raising my eyebrow, a smirk came across my face. I could tell he was thinking hard; the booze looked rather appealing to him, as if he really wanted to escape something. The guilty grimace he sported, twisted and lurched, contemplating on this apparent 'first.' "M-maybe a sh-shot, but th-that's it, okay?" I poured about an ounce and change into the empty glass and slid it closer to his side of the desk. "Th-th-th..." "Don't mention it." Gulping down a good swallow, I leaned back and gazed out of the window. "Y-you have a n-nice view f-f-from up-p here." Nothing but concrete with lights, sound, and movement. I saw nothing of value anymore. "Yeah, sure is." Taking another sip of cognac, I turned to face 97. Resting my arms on my desk, "You can pull up that collapsible stool." Confused, 97 looked around for a second, before, "In that corner there..." I pointed to a small nook near the foot of the bed. Eventually he found the item, unfolded it, and sat across from me at the desk. "F-f-fancy, g-guest seating!" "If you mock my meager existence, I'll beat you. With that said, you haven't touched your drink yet." His left eye blinked, followed by his right; mouth hanging open like a porn-star's. What an absolute wretch. Turning towards the window again,

I took a long drag from my cig, finished off my glass, and exhaled into the dark above.

"Before we even get started, I owe you this," I stated, sliding a small data-block towards him. He didn't touch it. He just looked at it, then back at me. "Wh-what's this f-f-for?" "It's ten grand..." "Wh-what?!" he verbally ejaculated. "Th-that's a l-lot of-f money! What, h-how, b-but you..." "Shut up and take it. Curden gave me a payout, and you deserve that. So, take it while I'm feeling generous." An emaciated hand protruded from his insectoid silhouette. Taking the device in his crickety grabber, he withdrew it into himself, and hid it away. "I-I've never h-had th-that much m-money..." Exhaling smoke through my nostrils, I looked over at him, and with a shit-eating grin, "Yeah, me neither."

"You're supposed to drink that, so you can handle what I've been, and will be, telling you." My eyes went from the cup to his face and back again several times. "Y-your e-eyes are b-" Like lightning, I threw my shades on so fast, it caused an audible disturbance in the air. "They're nothing. And you better not '*re-re-remember*' any detail about me. That's the kind of information people look for. Your coat is a clear (ha!) indicator of who you are; it's too unique. Your bottle-specs need to go, too." Putting the cigarette out in the overflowing ashtray, I exhaled out of the side of my mouth. Maybe if I'm not such a dick constantly, he'll do what I say. Maybe. "And now, you have the means to procure yourself a nice array, a plethora, if you will, of alternative articles of clothing that would better suit your career." Somehow, his mouth opened even wider and his eyes were so far out of his skull they were fogging up the lenses of those glasses. "No? Big words don't do it for ya either, kid?" Was there something wrong with him? "Are you retarded? 97? Hey!" He sat up straight, "S-sorry. Hey, l-l-look, wh-what's the p-plan?" Fair enough question, I did call him out for something. "Alright, look: Curden gave me the details on another deal. We need to get there at ten PM tomorrow night." 97 interjected, "B-but why s-so early?" Pouring myself another drink, "He wants us there to sign for the cargo before it goes to the docks. There's more money to be made if the process goes fast; is essentially what Curden told me. Here's another thing: Viizor™ is the one purchasing this cargo from Xiotron©®™SM. Viizor™ is, and I'm speculating, manufacturing Phyx® offworld. So, they're purchasing whatever that cargo is, getting us to sign off on it with Xiotron©®™SM, which grants them port-authority to bypass anymore security checks. The scam, it seems, is to get some illegal item offworld, and to pay the cops off to do it. We just have no idea what that cargo is, no idea who is behind this, how far up the corporate ladder it goes, or practically anything beyond what I just told you." If I opened a new pack of cigs now, and kept it as my house-pack, I could keep these last two in my coat for a rainy day. There's no logic in this, it just helps me cope with the fact that I told myself that I'd quit after I smoked that pack. So, I won't finish it just yet. Unwrapping the cellophane packaging, I smacked the new box on my palm to pack the tobacco a bit tighter. Pulling one from the cluster, I prepared to spark the lighter. "Oh, and Curden is a corrupt bastard; that's fucking addicted to the product the company he works for is selling." - *flick* -

97 grabbed his liquor glass with both hands and pulled it back to his lap, proceeding to then stare at it for a moment. After a bit, he looked up at me. "A-and? Wh-what d-does that mean?" "Means that Curden is bought out by Viizor™. Or Xiotron©®™℠, who knows. More than likely, it's Viizor™, but, that company is owned by

Xiotron©®™℠, so, in the end, it's all the same pyramid." "A-and we're g-g-going to... wh-what?" "And, *I'm* going to dispense justice. You can join me if you feel up to it, but I'm giving you a way out now." Smoke hovered around the dimly-lit desk. We stared at eachother across the glossy, faux-wood plane. "D-details. I n-need d-d-details." Leaning back to recline a bit, I sipped my drink. "I'm going to ambush the cargo team when I go to sign for it at the warehouse. I'm getting there early, way early. I should get there right as the transport team arrives, meaning, there will be a window between transports, where it'll just be the guys I'm supposed to meet, and possibly their escorts. If I'm lucky, there won't be many. I can finally find out what's in those crates that has everyone out for blood. Hopefully, I can get to the bottom of this. Either way, I'll be wanted for vigilantism or something in the next forty-eight hours." At the end of a long drag, I sighed heavily, expelling smoke into an already hazy room. 97 was shaking a little bit. He looked down at his glass, then back at me, then back at the glass. In a quick motion, he downed the shot. Too bad it had to go so quick; that was a fine year.

"O-okay, b-but what's i-in it f-for me? I'm n-not just g-going to th-throw my l-l-life away f-for n-nothing. The o-only reason I t-t-took the first sh-shady assignment is b-because I th-thou-ought I could get p-promoted. I needed eh-extra money. I didn't th-think it w-would lead t-to all of th-th, g-god dam-m-mit, th-this is bullshit!" Shockingly, he broke down crying. 97, sobbing into his hands, "Y-you have n-no idea h-how b-b-badly I w-want t-t-to die! I c-can't g-get a normal j-job. C-Curden helped g-get me th-this gig." Well, they say there are two sides to every story; and mine, is just one. Whatever Curden was up to by hiring this kid, it wasn't honest. "I bet he's using you. He pulled your ass off of the office grindstone, promised you more money, and got you to do whatever he wanted. Did I miss anything?" The kid was still weeping into his empty glass, held by both hands, as he buckled over into his own lap. "E-everyth-thing's-ss-so h-h-hard..." A torrential downpour of emotional distress came streaming from his pursed eyes. "Th-they never re-reissued m-me a g-gun, either. I-I d-don't qua-qualify..." A puzzled look struck my face, "What do you mean 'didn't qualify'? Didn't you say you were the top in your class or some shit?" "I-I was t-t-too nervous! A-and I was the only one in m-m-my c-class. No one wants to volunteer to be a GDC clerk. I needed the money-" "You're a fucking clerk?!" I heavily placed the glass on the desk. Again with the waterworks, "Y-yes! I-I'm s-s-s-sorry!" I sat back for moment while 97 dehydrated himself. Reaching for a new bottle of cognac, "Well, that's all beside the point; whose side are you on? The side of justice, or the system?" "A-are you a f-f-fuckin' terrorist n-now?!" 97 jolted back a bit in his stool. Exhaling with a jovial chuckle,

"Ha, no, you moron. Those people tried to kill us, remember? As far as I'm concerned, we're on our own side." Ashing the cig in the tray, "You're looking a little dry after your dam broke; want another round? It's on the house."

Knock – knock

A banging at my chamber door? Who the fuck could this be? I didn't order *Nü-dL*®; or did I? Am I drunk? "O-oh, g-g-god! Th-they f-f-found us!" wept 97 as he fell to the ground, seemingly preparing to accept death. "Shut up!" I hushed, drawing my weapon, and making my way quickly to the peep-hole. Standing with both feet shoulder-width apart was a woman dressed all in black with a large black sun-hat. I couldn't get a good look at her through the door. Slowly, I cracked the door, and peeked around it. "Tracy?" She looked at me in an astonished way, as she apparently wasn't paying attention. Her neon orange bob-cut gave it away. She was wearing a black blouse-jacket with a matching wiggle-skirt extending to her knees, ending in a flare. The blouse sleeves went down to about her elbows, and she was wearing small, black gloves, that came just below the wrist on the hand. She had fine stockings on with conservative black wedged shoes. Void-black lipstick graced her once rosy face. Sharp black cat-eye shades covered her bionic eyes. A large, wide-brimmed black sun-hat crowned this morose ensemble. In a very feminine smoker's voice, "It's Trish, now." My left eyebrow raised quite a bit, and I'm sure the rest of my face made a notable contortion. She pushed passed me and started looking around. "Nice place, John. Well, are ya gonna stand there with your dick in your hand, or are you gonna offer a lady a smoke?" I pointed at the desk behind her, "Help yourself, toots." Lifting her lip slightly, she tongued her incisor, making a sucking sound as she did it. Turning on her toe, she went for the open pack. From a small black bag attached to her hip, which I didn't see earlier, she produced a little telescopic cigarette holder. Fully extending it, she stuffed a dart in the wide end. Twisting to contrapposto, left hand on her hip, right holding the smoking-stick up in the air; as a philosopher upon a revelation. "Light, John?"

flick - "Alright, *Trish*, what can I do for you?" Sitting down, I poured myself another round. Exhaling, she looked around for a moment. "You can sit there, don't mind him; he can sit on the floor." "Thanksss..." She brushed the stool off with her free hand, "*Eww*, ew." Muttering under her breath. Clambering to sit upright, 97 had to take a moment to readjust himself. He looked up at Tracy, "Wh-what're y-you?" "Out of your league..." She ashed her cigarette on his forehead. "So, Johnny, regarding what I'm here for: I'd like to thank you for my freedom, first off, and secondly, I'd like to thank you for my new wardrobe. Your generous compensation of my time is greatly appreciated. However, because you made me aware of just how repulsive my previous occupation was, I'd like to request that you employ me. My rent is taken care of, I just need income. You know, for leisure activities." I finished my drink. "Alright, you can help me when I need you. Can you use a gun?" "I can download several new programs that were previously unavailable to me. Teehee." Cocking her head to the side, she kissed the air. "Interesting. Alright, well, go home and download all the naughty files, and meet me by the lift at six PM tomorrow. Got it?" She exhaled in a slow manner, keeping a fog about her face. "Sounds good, I'll see you tomorrow." Getting up to leave, she expertly put one foot before the other and approached the door. "And, Johnny," opening the door, she turned to look at me, "maybe you could reconsider, you know, about us?" "No amount of technological witchcraft is going to turn you into a real boy, Pinocchio. I suggest you bark up another tree, Tracy, you're just going to hurt yourself." She turned to leave, but quickly spat back, "It's *Trish*." With that, the door shut, and I could hear her angry clomping fading from ear-shot down the hallway.

"So, how's about it, kid; want to go down an irredeemable path and possibly die for vast sums of fiat currency?" Reclaiming his seat, he put his glass on the table. "I g-guess, p-pour me an-nother." I obliged him. "Here's to the end, partner."

Chapter 12

Wind; what was *wind*? Was it the passing of air over a moving surface? Where did it originate from; what blew the first gust? I get the chemistry of it; hot air/cold air, on a large scale, yada yada, I get all that. But, I wonder where it all comes from. What controls it all. You're raised in nothing but a scientific system, nothing has any life beyond the mechanical. Produce – Consume – Produce – Consume; it won't stop. Life has become a cancer and I refuse to believe it was always like this. You're told that the extinction of vast ecosystems that 'plagued' this planet were mere obstacles in the ever-expanding footprint of 'progress.' What if there was something greater than all of the mundane mechanisms and systems? Guess I wouldn't know until I went through the veil, huh? My lungs excised a cloud of smoke into the air which was dissipated into that powerful wind I was rambling about. God, I love the sound of this car.

Tracy was holding her giant hat on with her right hand, whose arm she had propped on the windowsill. Smoking with her left; leaving small, black lip-prints on the butt. Long, slender legs protruded from the end of her wiggle-skirt; like two bendy-straws in a wine-flute. She had swapped the dark hose for some black fishnet-stockings. I glanced over to see the red-glare of the cigarette reflecting off of her shades. Smirking, "Fishnets, huh?" "Some habits die hard, John," she exhaled into the breeze. "I've got something for your trouble..." I reached over to hand her a small finance block. She took it from my hand, "What's this?" "It's ten grand." "Wow... Th-thanks, Johnny! That's a fat wad'a cash, where'd ya get it?" "Don't ask questions. Just understand that I appreciate your assistance. Also, you're going to need a gun tonight; are you armed?" "Only with the knowledge of half the world's Elite CRTF™ teams!" Corporate Rights Task Force™: if a corporation had a situation it needed to settle – and no litigation or lawyering could fix it – they would declare an *'infringement of Corporate Rights,'* and send in a CRTF™. They are mostly comprised of mercenary-style guys, not usually Global Coalition Forces©, GCF© for the clowns, but the government does assist from time to time. It's all fucked. I'm not sure how she obtained manuals like that, but, hey, I had to follow my own rules and not ask questions. Taking a drag and nodding in approval, "Alright, that'll work."

We pulled off the highway into District 20A – comprised of the lower forty stories of the main city centre. There were enough interlocking roadways, starting around the thirty-ninth floor, to see the clear distinction in the upper and lower cities. 20A1; that was the designation of the Upper City district. Like a canopy of trees blocking the sun from all the shorter plants; or so I've read. Everything else seemed ground level; except that district. Prostitution was the leading industry in 20A; you could find almost anyone, or anything, selling itself in public display. The district was mostly too poor to afford policing, so only a few areas were really safe to go to at any given time. The Big Corps didn't seem to mind this slum, slap-dab in the inner sprawl of Metropol 20. Probably because this place had a high output of new 'citizens' every other fiscal. 20A was the victim of having the highest density population to space ratio in the entire city; which meant higher consumers per capita. It was the origin-point for the city, and all construction moved in a circular grid extending out from this centre point. 'A' was the Old District, 'historical,' as they say. It was a rundown shit-hole, stuffed to the brim with the worst anarchist scum imaginable. How the fuck did 97 come from *this* ghetto? Pimps, pushers, users, thugs; all out to make their cut, all ready to leave your bullet-ridden carcass in an alley. And, oh, how many alleys there were in this ancient place. Rumor had it, 20 was one of the oldest Metropols still in use; and after traveling around here long enough, you start to believe it. You can't really tell anymore, though: the sprawl keeps growing every day.

Flipping the lights on, we descended into the depths of the old city. It was perpetually dark down here and street-lamps ran 24/7. The Pharmaceutical Industry loved this area of town; the sheer number of repeat customers alone – and the fresh cases appearing daily – didn't exactly hurt business. Viizor™, BioDyme®, and the Met-20 Homebrew – CryoCom©: they have no issue testing their products on the residents of this place; and the abominations left in the wake of their medical experiments could be seen shambling about the streets. Their contorted, mangled bodies – simply vessels for deranged and traumatized minds. It would be humane to just shoot them. And that was just a handful of the major players. Tech companies like BellEnd™ or LGB&T® let loose with all the most invasive and addictive gadgets the mind could conjure up. Big Food was probably the worst. They fed the population the nastiest slop, wrapped in a bow and served like a real turkey dinner. Beil™ & Syk™ ® was probably the worst company operating in the local area regarding the 'food' industry. There was a *B&S* food market on every block, and every other product in other stores had a *B&S* sticker. So much for a 'free and open' market.

"I hear that the city Alphas in every Metropol are like this one," exhaled Tracy. Seemed legit. Ground-zero for all the worst that the city had to offer. All the new tech, all the new diseases, the chemicals, brainwashing, re-processed water, recycled air… All the big corps would assess the damage on the population of 20A like they did in all the Alpha blocks, from what I hear. It only makes sense; the population was the most dense and it had a high birthrate. Essentially, they could farm their test subjects. It also allowed for opportunities to test on the issue of genetic problems of their products; as there was very little generational turn-around time. Thinking about it made me sick. Sick in the way the air smelled around this place. Pollution was bad here just from the congestion of people; but 20B was still worse, as it was almost exclusively industrial. And I wasn't rich enough to go offworld, so there was never any reason to go there.

I rarely leave 20C unless it's to work or go on assignment. It's shit, but it's bearable. One day, I'll get a place in 21, overlooking one of the farming districts of 22. Wouldn't that be the day. Then I wouldn't have to go anywhere, really. I don't even offer rides to people, ever. The only reason I agreed to pick 97 up was that his place was in the same district as the warehouse we needed to be at. I pulled onto his street and slowed down, looking for the exact building. Everything was dilapidated, crumbling around us. Debris from old brick structures piled along the walls of alleyways; trash blew across the streets with the few gusts of wind that managed to penetrate the hollowed-out shell of looming highways. Like a mushroom, the Mega Passes created a network over us, blotting out almost all daylight. The joke there is that there isn't any daylight in the first place, "Haha..." "What are you laughing about, Johnny?" I'm starting to lose it. "Nothing; keep an eye out for 97, he'll be w-" "Oh look! There he is! Harry, hey, HiFi!!" Tracy was waving frantically as we pulled up to the curb. He stood there in his sticky-looking, plastic coat. Pushing up on his glasses with a single, bony finger, his gaze changed from ground to us. I should hit him with the car and end his suffering.

Turning to Tracy, I had a look of bewilderment on my face; I probably looked like I thought she was retarded. "Are you short-circuiting?" I asked, wearing a puzzled expression. She snapped, "What? Don't be an ass. Harold Flynn – *Hi Fi...*" "Alright, I already regret unlocking your systems, good fucking g-" "H-h-hey f-fellas!" Both Tracy and I turned to look at 97, each sporting an equally disgusted but amused look. "Get the fuck in, shut and listen the fuck up." I pealed out, off down the street.

"Automota, engage auto-pilot, and don't kill us." "*Ooh yeah, you're in my hands now, baby. Just sit back and enjoy the ride...*" Taking my hands off the steeringwheel, I turned to the centre of the car. "Listen, we're going to arrive in a few minutes, and I'm going to ask you one last time; if you want out, this is your last chance." 97 was grabbing the back of his head, tapping the floor with both feet. Tracy was seductively licking her lips. "I'll take that as compliance. When we pull up, I'm going to give you two some toys and we're going to spring a trap on these gangsters, yeah? Hopefully, no one gets plugged and we can all walk away with some interesting stories, and probably some serious reward money after we loot the place and bail. We'll say terrorists came again, and I'll put the blame on Curden. Maybe we can keep going up the ladder if they decide to sack Curden for incompetence." 97 piped up, "O-o-okay, b-but I'll n-n-need m-more m-money..." "Yeah, yeah, we all do, don't worry, we'll work on that later." We pulled into a dark, cluttered alley. "On the other side of this block is the warehouse. Ready?" We all exited the vehicle and I signaled for them to come around back. "Pop the trunk..." "*Oooh, yesss, daddy...*" -*kuchunk*- Letting out a heavy sigh, I reached for a cigarette. -*flick*- "Alrighty then..." Rummaging around, I pulled out two six-shooter pistols. "You two can have these, and there's plenty of ammo in the trunk here." Reaching back into the cargo space, my hand gripped the cold steel of... "That's a T&T™ BlastDaddy© Express!! Wow!" 97 exclaimed, stumbling forward a bit to get a better look. He was right to be impressed; it was a serious piece of artillery. The Titus & Titan™ BlastDaddy© Nitro Express XD was a rifle stacked on an over-under shotgun. Sounds ridiculous, because it is. It was a triple-stack over-under, breach-loading war crime. It could hold one .700 Nitro Express round and two 12 gauge rounds. Pulling a bandoleer laden with shotgun and high-caliber rifle rounds out from my mobile armoury, I closed the lid. Draping the bandoleer around myself, I motioned for the other two to follow me. "Hey, Johnny, I know a guy right around the block, I worked for him right after I was manufactured. Don't start the fireworks without me, 'kay?" Tracy blew me a kiss and then skipped off around the corner. "Are you fucking kidding me..." Aloud, I proclaimed my disbelief. "M-more m-money for us, r-r-right?" The kid looked at me, seeking approval. Nodding, I turned to push onwards down the alley.

Taking the safety off my one-man-revolution, we proceeded to creep down the narrow, dank gully. Patches of asphalt that had broken away with wear revealed stone-work beneath. Rancid, stagnant cesspools of run-off, gathered in the eroded and damaged potholes dotting the road. The buildings went all the way up to the canopy of mega passes; with all manner of interconnecting bridges and rail lines. Numerous support beams and permanent scaffolding were erected over the centuries in order to manage the buckling weight of an even larger city above. Some shit was always falling, or raining, down upon you. Most people bring an umbrella when visiting 20A. Streams of blue, white, pink, and other coloured lights, shown through the artificially imposed darkness – casting all sorts of crazy patterns and shadows. The light played with the endless mists and drippings of the over-city. This was a nightmare to conduct espionage in. It was also a blessing.

Chapter 13

This might very well be the dumbest shit I've ever felt the need to do. I have no idea what I'm getting myself into. How many guards, how well armed, how well trained? Was I going to need to rub out the transit team too? What happens if soneone escapes, how much time do I have until Curden gets word and puts my name through processing? I'll be liquidated for sure. Not that I really mind death, but I definitely wasn't enticed by the idea of getting snuffed out by some kid who paid a company to fly drones for bounty-hunter gigs. That is probably the weirdest industry of the modern age: pay to punish. The Corps and government were so desperate for income that they outsourced execution. Now, any kid with access to their mom's PFC© can jump in an augmented reality console and, *'choose how to dispense the ultimate verdict!'* For just *99.95,* your child can know what it feels like to take a life. Regardless, I was about to be up against flesh, or at least metal; something tangible. I needed to assess the situation quick. I took it all in – there were numerous discarded piles of boxes, trashbags, and random debris. Large dumpsters lined the alley along the rear-entrances to various establishments, dwellings, and whatever else was entombed in these concrete pillars of Hades. Ahead, at the other end of the back-street was one of the warehouse walls.

"There're two security doors on our left, and I'm assuming they lead into the back offices of the warehouse," I stated, taking cover behind a dumpster with 97. "And, looks like there's a loading door at the end of the alley... but, it's a bit small. I don't think they would bring the crates in from that way." 97 was sweating, clasping his pistol with both hands. Reaching for my smokes, I remembered I had a new pack, and to not touch the 'final two.' I thought now would be as good a time as any, to have a smoke. "H-hey, c-c-can I g-grab one?" A puzzled look came across my face, as I turned to look at the kid.

"Alright, suit yourself." Shakily, he retrieved the cig. -*flick*-, I lit both of them, exhaled, then put the pack away. "You gonna be alright?" "I-I d-d-don't know m-man." "If you piss yourself, just stay a metre away from me." I turned back to examining our surroundings. There was a long line of industrial-type windows, lining the wall along part of the warehouse. "We need to move that dumpster, to right under that window." Pointing out what I meant to 97, he nodded slowly, and swallowed heavy. Moving out from behind our cover, we crept a few metres forward and came to another dumpster. "Alright," whispering. I shouldered my weapon, and crouched to push the dumpster. "On three..." 97 put his pistol in his waistband, like some fucking bandit, and dove in to help me out. Whatever that's worth, I supposed he tried, credit where it's due. "One... Two... Threeeehh!!" We pushed that thing, heavy as it was even with wheels, across the alley. I didn't think about how we were going to stop the dumpster's momentum before it crashed into the warehouse wall. Fuck.

An ear-shattering clattering of steel against concrete rang through the alley. An alert to everyone; we were there. Instinctually, I clamoured up onto the dumpster. Peering into the window, I could make out a large storage area with at least four-story-tall industrial shelving; all stocked full of crates and parts and items of all sizes. A few uniformed men were standing near a transport vehicle by an open cargo door on the wall furthest from me. I could only make out three, but one was shouting to someone, and pointing in this direction.. "Kid, hide behind this trash-wagon, someone's coming!" I hissed, crouching down on top of the dumpster. I put my rifle to the side, reached into my jacket, and pulled out a long, thin dagger. Holding it backwards in my right hand, I perched near the edge, overlooking the back-door. A few moments later, the sounding of the doorseals cracking let me know it was go-time. Like an ancient predator, I leapt onto my target before I, or he, even knew what the other looked like. My knife plunged deep into his chest, piercing a lung; I knew it. No sounds; that's how the Jaguar did it. A silent killer, my left hand covered the mouth of my prey. The blood he began coughing up splashed back into his face against my palm. Only a few more spasms and it would all be over.

I assisted the twitching, exsanguinated figure to the ground. "97, get the door, now!" I softly yelled, motioning to the slightly open entrance. He hurried over and caught the door then crouched near the entrance, holding it open. "Wh-wh-what the f-f-!?!" I interjected, "This is serious shit. We're all in, remember?" "F-fuck, m-man..." Worthless. Retrieving my big-gun from the dumpster-top, I shouldered it again and prepared to go inside. "Ready?" I looked down at 97. "Kill everyone in there.

We can figure out how to address the whole thing after; this is our only shot... GO!"

Rushing into the warehouse, I took cover behind the first wall of cargo. It was decent cover, but I'd have to keep moving. "Flank around that side, and stay low," I harshly whispered, motioning to 97 to go around the back while I approached from the front. Getting to the edge of the cargo-wall, I peeked through a few mechanical parts. I noticed the three men were still standing there, talking. One was a Xio, seemingly the one doing the yelling earlier. He was relatively tall for his kind, thin and gangly. The other two were normal enough, both brunette dudes, average height, buff. All were in the same black uniforms as the guy I just dispatched. I could make out 'Xitran®' on the arm patch. Xitran® was a local logistics subsidiary of Xiotron©®™SM Met20 Holding Co.™, so I knew this was the worst mistake I was about to make... if I fucked up. I had to make sure everyone got whacked, or I'd never be able to fix this scene.

Using the trusty iron-sights, I lined up a shot. My finger licked at the trigger, ready to start the festivities. Taking a drag from the dangling cig in my mouth, I held my breath... A deafening explosion – a bright, crimson spray, violently coated everything in a three metre vicinity of the spindly Xio. His body, torn in twain; legs crumpled in a heap where they stood – torso a metre away, thrown from the concussive force of the blast. The look on his mangled face, from what I could tell, was one of bewilderment. He was caught entirely off-guard. No movement; his soul was ejected at warp-speed. I barely recovered from the first shot when lead started to hail on my position. Ducking behind a large steel crate, I cracked the breech and loaded another Express round. Before I could think of a counter attack, four gunshots rang out from a different direction. One of the remaining Company men was screaming, he was probably hit. Now was my chance. Finger on the trigger, I whipped around from the cargo-wall at full speed,

"AAHHHHH!!" – I let loose with a high-explosive shotgun round. 'Didn't realize how close I was to the guy when I pulled the trigger. Right in the gut. His body exploded like a piñata packed with C4. 97 came running from down a cargo aisle. "O-oh, oh, f-f-fu...!" "Now isn't the time, finish that guy off. I'll go check the transport truck for anyone else!" Walking over to the cab of the loader, I noticed how high-tech and new the vehicle was. CryoCom© decals? What was Viizor™ transporting that required cryo-tech? Was this the chemical container for Phyx© ingredients? I had so many questions, but I needed to secure the area before I could ask any more.

The door to the driver's-side of the loader cab was wide open. I was approaching it from the rear, so I shouldered my weapon on the left; every tiny edge helps. Peeking into the crew carriage, I covered a figure with the sights of my gun. He froze, one hand in the glove-box, and looked straight at me.

He was sprawled out on the bench-seat, desperately reaching for whatever was in that compartment. His eyes were green and his hair a dirty blonde. He looked at me, chest rising and falling with each adrenaline-boosted breath. I'd say he was maybe 18 or 19; a young kid. Fear gripped his face, mutilating a youthful facade with a tormented grimace. Nothing really quite hits you in the same way as when you see an inevitable finality suck the vigor and idealism from a youthful soul.

All the windows in the cabin of the loader had fractured and blown outward from the pressure of the enclosed blast. I hope CryoCom® approves of this new red paint-job. Looking around for a second, I noticed a holopad on the floor. Picking it up, I saw that it was the manifest for the cargo. Walking back toward the rear of the vehicle, "We must have just arrived when the transit guy showed up... 97?" I looked up to see 97 standing next to the body of the man he shot during the skirmish. A small, black knife was protruding from the mercenary's right eye-socket. "Why the silent kill? 97?" A tear rolled down his pursed face as he turned to look at me. "Hey, I know it's hard. But, listen; this manifest states that the cargo is cryo-frozen... hominids, property of Xiotron©®™℠." My face went white with shock. Hominid means ape, and last I checked, the various human races were the only apes still in existence. I really hope there aren't people in this transport... Grabbing a crow-bar off the back of the vehicle, I leapt into the cargo bed. Prying, stabbing; I was opening one of these crates. Ripping the wooden casing away from the steel frame enclosed within, I revealed a block of four Cryo-Pods©. I'm assuming each crate had four pods. Luckily, each of these has a digital read-out of the contents. According to the manifest, the maintenance access code is 8-3-0-0-1...

Plugging that combination into the first tube's on-board computer, the information made my stomach jump to my throat.

Specimen 33-00045926

Europid, Female, AB-

Age: 13

"No..." escaped my lips as I quickly moved to the next...

Specimen 33-00045927

Asian, Female, B+

Age: 8

...and the next...

Specimen 33-00045928

Europid, Male, O-

Age: 11

...it can't be...

Age: 5

Age: 12

Age: 7

Age: 4

Seinman didn't say, 'kits in the crate.', he said 'kids…' "Kids in the crate." I needed to sit down. The missing kids, abducted by Xiotron©®™℠? A major corporate kidnapping ring? But why? What the fuck is the benefit of this? Curden must have known. Hopping down from the bed of the loader, "97, Curden had to have known about what was being shipped, there's no way he didn't. We have to stop him! Do you hear me?! Curden is a child-trafficker! And if he's not the guy, he certainly works for them and we need to put a stop to it. There's no getting rich off this type of cargo, this is beyond fucked up! 97? Hey, I'm talki-" "Y-you're always t-t-talking!" he yelled, echoing through the warehouse. Without turning around, he turned his head to the side. "D-don't you th-think th-there's anoth-ther angle to th-this? L-let's l-look the other w-way, John; C-Curden is off-ffering us a l-lot of money if-ff w-we do th-this, right? W-well, I n-need money, J-John. She's r-real s-sick." "Who's sick?" "M-my m-m-mother.

She n-needs a l-lot of h-help. And I c-can't aff-fford it with-thout p-playing a b-bit dirty." "What are you saying, Harry?" "L-l-look th-the other way J-John... J-Just f-forget wh-what's in th-the c-crates." The whole fucking world was against me. Before I could reach for my pistol, Flynn had drawn on me with lightning speed. "And it's n-n-ninety-sev-ven, t-to you."

How could I have been this caught off-guard? This little bastard has the balls to pull a gun on me?! Who the fuck saw that coming? I should have hit him with the car. What the fuck was I going to do? My eyes darted in all directions. "N-n-no, n-no, you f-fucker! Y-you h-haven't a c-clue..." 97 rambled on for a minute or so about his sick mother; bed ridden in that ghetto we picked him up at. He needed a lot of money, and took the job when Curden offered him something on the side *if he played ball*. He was supposed to sign the documents. That was it; no questions, no inspections, sign and look away. Flynn said he was under the impression that our assignments were legit, until the night we survived the attack at the hangar-bay. He said he felt trapped, nervous, desperate. He needed money and thought if he got Curden arrested for corruption, that he could get a promotion and a raise. I was supposed to be the way out of his issues or, at least, the way to more money to assist in getting rid of them. That's why he agreed to come with me the day he confided in me about having suspicions about Curden. But, he knew as well as I did that revealing this whole thing probably meant we would be killed or, at the worst, rendered destitute and hopeless. And, when the adrenaline wore off, that just wasn't going to fly for Harold Flynn. How I overlooked that he was a desperate man on the edge was beyond me. To be fair, I never really gave him a moment to speak; and why would I? It took six years for him to get a paragraph out. But that didn't matter currently;

I was the one facing the business-end of the gun.

He was crying, teeth bared; gnashing as he spit his venom about all the wrongs he had suffered in life. Pistol shaking, his voice began escalating to a scream, and his posture became sloppy, contorted. Inching a little closer to me, "S-so, y-y-you, are g-gonna f-fu-f-fucking sign th-the manifest! Or I'll f-f-fucking kill you!" His eyes darted to the digi-pad in my hand. A frown crept across my troubled face. He couldn't see my eyes, but he could definitely see my expression. "D-do it!" *BANG* – I audibly sighed when I realized I wasn't hit. 97 had fired off to the side but had the gun trained again on me in a millisecond. "N-N-NNNOOWWWWW!!!" he screamed at the top of his lungs. Bits of spittle launched from his frothing, toothy, feral mouth. Standing up straight, a blank look took hold of me. I tossed the manifest tablet down at the ground so that it slid towards him upon impact. Tears continued to stream down his face.

"I-I'm s-s-sorry, J-John..." Silence hung in the air like a thick fog, clogging my ability to draw even a single breath.

– BANG –

Chapter 14

Glass, when it shatters, creates thousands of tiny shards, all reflecting light at different angles. As they fall, they produce the most wondrous colours. I can almost hear the twinkling, clinking sound of crystal. The concussive force of the bullet's impact obliterated 97's thick glasses; sending pieces flying in all directions. Skull and brain fragments, having been evicted from the remainder of Harry's cranial cavity, scattered across the warehouse floor beside him. Crashing to the ground, his limp corpse was as motionless as I was. Blood began to pool immediately around what remained of his head, gushing from openings both natural and man-made. I went to reach for my gun again... "Ah, ah, ahh... Not on my watch, big man," came a seductive, feminine voice that sounded eerily familiar.

"Mhmm, ladies and gentlemen, don't touch that dial." The militant gracefully walked around from the other side of the loading vehicle. Clacking as they went, her combat boots looked beaten and worn. Her uniform was a tattered green jumpsuit with a black back-pack. It had all sorts of little gadgets hanging off of it. She was sporting a black balaclava with only her mouth and eyes showing. Her lips were a ruby red and her eyes were an emerald green. What I was most worried about, however, were the black, leather gloves holding the semi-automatic rifle – which was pointed at me. "Alright, spill the beans, you have me, you coulda killed me if ya wanted to..." I wasn't in the mood for subtlety. The softest threat was offered in return. "You're right, I could've killed you. Here, yesterday, maybe the day before that. But I didn't, so you're going to give me what I want in return." My patience was wearing thin with this ever-expanding bullshit. "Or?" "Or I'll shoot you? Haha, come on, *baby*, you didn't think I was just going to let some *cop* off the hook, right?"

Three more heavily armed thugs flanked behind her, checking her perimeter. Lowering her weapon, I felt safe enough to get inquisitive. "I know you, don't I?" -*flick*- "Probably not," she exhaled, "but we've met, heh." There's no way. How could she have known where I was? Before I could inquire about who she was, she went to speak with one of the newly arrived thugs. "Hey, how the fuck did you find this place?" Giggling, she looked over at me, and said mockingly, "If you must know, we had a tracker on you. Some detective you are, Agent Peiler. Ha!" Tracker? When was I in contact with anyone recently? Did they track the car? Fuck, did they fuck up my car?! "Hey, if you fucked with my car, I swear to g-" "You'll do what? Throw a hissy-fit? Shut the fuck up, pig, no one asked you to squeal, yet." Turning back around, she returned to her other discussion. "You're terrorists, aren't you?" No answer. "Well, aren't you?!" She turned her head to look in my direction. "That's a matter of perspective, honey." Strutting towards me, she got uncomfortably close to my face. Wrong move. Whispering to me in a soft, creamy voice, "And from my perspective, you're the terrorist. But hey, thanks again for the smoke." As she turned on her heel to leave, I seized upon the opportunity she so carelessly provided. "Hmmph!!" My hand went over that serpentine mouth as I pulled her to my chest and planted my pistol to her temple. "I'd blow your fucking brains out right now if you weren't still useful, bitch." Her compatriots simultaneously pointed their weapons at us, trying to get a clear shot at me. At least I had a pretty good shield.

Frantically, I pointed my six-shooter from one fiend to the next. "So, what's *your* safeword?" I muttered into her knit-covered ear. She growled a bit. "Now, while we're all in this standoff, you're going to tell me just exactly how you managed to track me." Resentfully, the woman spat out,

"When you presented your cigarette pack to me, I slipped the tracker in it. Hahaha, I didn't think you'd have kept the pack *this* long." Holy shit. "You looked like a pig from the moment I saw you, that's why I jumped. But I thought, *nah, he's not here for me, he's here for the Xio*. And I was right, *Johnny*." "Then you knew what he was up to?" "Listen, cop, the Underground has been following Seinman for months, trying to figure out what he's up to. We gathered a shit-tonne of info from him. We wanted to know what was being shipped, where and why. And you found the bigger picture to it all." What did she mean by this? "How do you mean 'the bigger picture?'" "You left all of his documents; it outlines a big Corporate program to use citizens as fuel for the drug industry," she started struggling a little bit. "You bastards destroyed a shipment of kids a week or so back, you know that? Do you?! I saw it happen! I didn't know that's what was in those crates and neither did you fuckers! Some fucking intel! This is why no one sympathizes with your cause, because you're indiscriminate with your violence! You're no better than the tyrants in their neon towers! Fuck you!" I tightened my grip around her neck. "I was there too, fed! The plan got all fucked up, none of that was supposed to happen. Everything went wrong, okay? My own sister died that night! Shot in the head and left in the alley like some fucking trash! This is war! Shit gets fucked up!" 'Sister'... I couldn't help but think of that young girls face; lying there in the gutter, her porcelain flesh painted with mascara and blood. My face was expressionless aside from the wide-eyed stare I had adopted. Her eyes became wide. Incoherently, she cursed and wriggled in my grasp. With the butt of my pistol's grip, I punched that working girl's clock. Instantly, she went limp; out cold.

One by one, my assailants tightened their aim on me. My hostage's now-limp form offered less protection than its rigid and flailing counterpart. Great, I should have just dragged her, kicking and screaming. My backstabbing, sniveling partner's brains were splattered all over the floor not even two metres from my right. The loading truck was to my left, and I might be able to make a break for the cover it provided. It was the only close barrier between myself and the eco-warriors... "Hey, fuckers!" a high-pitched voice echoed from across the warehouse. Everyone looked, myself included. Before anyone could get a look at what or who, a hail of bullets rained down on those goons. They all dropped to the ground, trying to crawl away, while getting cut to pieces by machinegun-fire. I ducked around behind the loader. Careful not to take any stray rounds to the ass, I positioned myself behind the massive rear-left tire. Propping my unconscious prisoner up against the tire, I pulled some zip-restraints from inside my jacket. Now arrested and knocked the fuck out, I felt it was safe to say she may be a neutralized threat.

Peeking out from behind my safety, I saw the men had all been slaughtered. Blood was everywhere flowing from pool to pool and forming interconnecting streams. A couple guys were twitching and trying to move, but it was a hopeless effort. They outstretched their hands, but found nothing to grasp. Curling in on themselves, clutching at their wounds; wailing, swearing, weeping. The pools and streams connected, bit by bit, and soon the whole area around them was coated in a smooth crimson gloss. But, who the fuck...? I turned my head to look around for the phantom gunner. Sliding down a ladder to a catwalk was, I was assuming, Tracy. As she began trotting towards me, waving her hand; I noticed she was carrying a sizeable weapon. It looked like an old M60, and she had ammo-belts draped around her shoulders and neck. The gun was hanging from a strap on her right. It was an odd spectacle.

"I thought I told you to wait until I got back?" Starting in on me as soon as she got close, "'*Download da files t' be da best warrior, Twish. Oops, we did da whole t'ing wit'-out'cha.*' That's you, that's fucking you, Johnny. Prick." She started looking around at all the carnage. "There're bodies everywhere, and it looks like a couple different factions were involved." I looked sideways at her. "You don't say?" "Oh, snap," she exclaimed, "that's Harry, dead there. Oh, man, they shot him in the fucking head, would you look at that, wow." "They really never got the 'grief' emotion right with you things, huh?" -*flick*- Still striking that contrapposto pose, "So, what *did* happen to 'im?" "The assclown pulled a gun on me, and was about to fucking shoot me, until that chick," I motioned to the tied up gimp-in-terrorist's clothing, "decided to put one through his dome. Can't say I care much, but I was starting to like the kid." Exhaling, I went to search the bodies for anything useful. As I turned over corpse after cadaver, "You know, we need to get out of here quick, and we need to do something about those frozen kids. Can you muscle that crate off the loader?" Tracy stood back, eyeing up the task. "Not a chance, hun, I'm strong, but I'm not a forklift." That meant we'd have to take the loading vehicle or something. Fuck, what the hell am I supposed to do with all this fucking mess?

I guess at this point, I was a fugitive. We didn't have the technology on hand to unfreeze the kids and I couldn't get them off the truck either. We were fucked if we stayed around much longer, eventually the second loading team was going to show up... or maybe this was the second team? Regardless, there wasn't enough info to call this place secure, and it wasn't safe enough to wait around long enough to make an informed decision. "Tracy..." "*Trish.*"

"Whatever; are you able to drive that loader?" She looked at it, and walked around to the cabin door. "Are you fucking serious, Johnny?! Everything is drenched in blood and entrails, what the fuck happened here?!" "Yeah, shit, slipped my mind." Eyebrows slanted inward, face pursed; she didn't look happy. "I can drive this thing, but grab me one of those cargo-tarps; I'm not fucking my outfit up." Clicking my RemoteReturn© device on, (which switches the car's auto-pilot on, having it navigate to the nearest street access point; one of her best features) I set about gathering more items from the bodies. Guns, ammo, whatever I'd need to go rogue.

Automota pulled up a minute later to the open cargo door in front of the loader. Popping the trunk, I filled it with a bunch of goodies I had harvested from the boys. I grabbed another cargo-tarp, and threw it over the partially exposed cryo-tanks I had opened earlier. After having secured the tarp, I hopped down to reconvene with Tracy. "Alright, follow me, stay pretty close, but not on my ass; if you ding my fender, I'll deactivate you. We're going to drop this thing off at the hospital in 20B, then bail out." Those hollow, black eyes, zeroed in on me. "And then what, John? You didn't load your trunk up with an arsenal for no reason." Perceptive 'bot, she is. "You never know what you may need. You'll hop in my ride, and we'll figure stuff out from there. I don't think we can live normal lives anymore." "I was a mechanical prostitute, you fucking retard. I never lived a normal life." Heh, ain't that the truth. "And what about her?" Tracy pointed to the unconscious woman, still propped up against the loaders rear tire. "Oh, yeah, almost forgot about her. Here, help me put her in the front seat of my car." "Why the front?" "So I can see when she wakes up. I can't chance letting her get the jump on me." We tossed our captive in the passenger seat, buckled her in, and I put another restraint around her torso and the chair itself.

"Well, see you at the hospital. And thanks." I revved the engine a couple of times before pulling out into the street. Tracy followed in the loader, lumbering behind in the behemoth vehicle. I'm in for one hell of a night.

Chapter 15

-ring ring- "Whatt'you want, Johnny, you know not to bang my line 'less it's about money or coke... Haha! No, Johnny, no, I'm kidding; you know I'd never hang out with you of my own volition! Haha, OH! Yo, J-McDaddy, those stocks are lookin' good, real good. Speculative trading is going through the roof! Haha, so, what'd'ya fuck up?" "Listen Milt, you really need to get your intel straight. We walked into an ambush; the terrorists were waiting for us! They wasted everyone, even 97! I'm coming to your office now, I'll be there in a couple hours." "What the *FUCK* do you mean?! How the fuck did that hap-*tsssk-*" *-click-*

Hopefully he bought that bit. This was my only shot of getting close enough to Curden again. I needed to really think this through. There wasn't a whole lot I could do; Justice needed to be dealt. At least in this small way, some of those kids would be avenged. That greasy fuck! How could he do this, how could he be so soulless! His interior was as hideous as his exterior. There was no way he could go on getting away with it; I had to do something. "Uhh…" Oh, goddammit, this bitch is finally up.

"Good evening; if you make a funny move, I'll kill you, yeah?" "Uhhh… whaa…?" I waited for her to come-to a little more. "Uh, fuck, what happened, where..?!" The cold steel of my revolver-barrel pressed against the black knitting of the ski-mask right under her chin. "Listen, bitch, you're going to start talkin' right the fuck now, or I'll dump your carcass over the free-way *so* fuckin' fast you won't have time to scream. Get me?" Her eyes glanced over at me, and she attempted to nod as best as I'd let her. "Alright, and take that fucking thing off…" Reaching over, I pulled off the knit-mask. Long, brilliant red hair fell down around her shoulders in a haphazard way. Her matching lipstick was smeared a bit, but she wasn't wearing any other types of makeup to mess

up, aside from some lightly applied black eye-liner.
"So, you want to know the plan? Maybe you can tell
me what you know, too, then. Up until – however
long I was out – ago, I had no idea that
Xiotron©®™℠ and Viizor™ were using kids to
harvest the ingredients for Phyx©. I knew the
corporate plan, and the Undergrounds networks have
copied it and are spreading it around. Hopefully, we
can get some real support against the Corps." I didn't
even glance at her. "You're going to need an army to
take down the Mega Corps. They literally own and
operate this, and most, planets. Are you guys
insane?" She looked at me, smirking. "Are you? You
seem to be going pretty far off-mission there, Special
Agent. I can't imagine you're having that loader, with
all the cargo, following us because you intend to turn
it all in to your boss for a reward. No. I didn't think
so."Softly, she let out a feminine chuckle.

"Look, John, may I call you John? Anyway, listen, honey, if you want to know what I know, read these documents I have. After all, *you* found them." "And they are, where, exactly?" Seductively biting her lower lip, "In my jumper, wouldn't ya know? Oh, darn it..." You have to be fucking kidding me. Either I'm some magical lady-slayer; or this broad is gearing up to fucking slit my jugular. "You think I'm stupid enough to just let you kill me like that?" "Haha! Haa'yeah, yeah, I actually did." She giggled. Shaking my head, "I take it you enjoyed your undercover gig at the club?" "If you're gonna tie me up and verbally humiliate me, at least give me a cigarette." Sighing, I reached into my coat for the fresh pack of smokes. Placing one between her lips, I put the pack in the cup holder, incase this discussion got heavy. "So, these documents, if they're even real..." She was looking at me with a scornful gaze. "You need a light, too?" The cig dropped from her lips, "My hands are zip-tied behind my back. How the fuck am I supposed to do anything? Just untie me so I can huff a dart for Christ's sake." I chuckled. "You'd kill me immediately because you think I'm somehow responsible for your sisters death. I saw how you looked at me before I put you to sleep." "You were there, if anything I should just blame you for it outright and say you personally killed her." "Well, you'd be glad to know that, no, I didn't kill her. However, I know who did. Your sister attacked me after I shot her boyfriend. And before you flip about that, understand that he had a knife to me then-partner's throat. Naturally I mag-dumped at the first opportunity. She rushed me and took one to the back of the head." I could see the hatred, anguish, and longing manifest in every quivering wrinkle on her clenched face. Tears began to cascade down her cheeks in streaks of black. "Who did it... Who?!" she yelled through closed teeth. "You already enacted revenge when you blew Flynn's brains out. Thanks for that, I owe you one." I chuckled. She slumped back in the seat as tears continued to run down her face. I looked over at the pathetic insurgent. "Your sister was too young for a bar-code; what was she doing running ops for you lot?" "S-she was pulling her first mission, all she was supposed to do was be a lookout. I don't think it matters what I say at this point, so; Dillon was supposed to cut the power and emergency alert systems. But when we found them later that night in that alley, we knew they were murd-" "No, not in the least. We tried to walk past, but your friend wasn't having it, I guess trying to show-off to your sister. I'm assuming the power never got cut off because he stopped on the way to suck face. Then we stumbled along and he decided to pull a knife on us when I wanted to keep walking. Your friends are violent criminals you know." "God dammit..." she muttered under breath. Leaning on the passenger door, her weeping was soft enough to where the music drowned it out.

"Look, I need information, and I don't think we need to be enemies, at least right now." She looked at me, sniffling and wiping the tears from her eyes. Her makeup was smeared all over. "If I untie you, will you play ball?" This was a bad idea. "I don't really have a choice currently, I'd say." Holding up a knife in my right hand, "I'll stab yo-" "Yeah, yeah, yeah, please, I get people off saying shit twice as raunchy." I cut her loose.

-flick- "So, first off," she exhaled, "I wasn't 'undercover,' *smart guy*, that's my job; I'm a dominatrix..." "You're a gimp with titties for masochists; don't sugar coat it." Glaring at me and inhaling, "As I was saying; I didn't know who to go to about all the sick things I found out just by being in that work place. The patrons, if you will, had a number of shady, evil actors in their midst. And I needed to find an outlet. Luckily I found the Underground, and I've been with them for some

245

time-" "I asked for information, not your life story. Pony up those documents you were yammering on about." Huffing, "Fine." She reached into her jumpsuit and pulled out that manila envelope, the one I had found back at the club. I can't believe I forgot that piece of evidence during my murder-induced adrenaline high. "I got to keep the original copy," she boasted, "but, here, there's a digital version in the envelope." Snatching it from her, I quickly removed the digital chip, and placed it in Automota's drive. After a couple of moments, *"This is pretty serious info, J. Want me to have it dictated?"* "Sure, we've got a bit of a drive anyway."

"Protocols of the Shareholders of Xiotron©®™℠: Dictate 1194: It is with great elation that the Board of Directors issues this company edict, in which shall be secured permanent market stability for almost all sectors of corporate holdings.

"Issue 1 – Concerning Viizor™ and associated subsidiaries; The Objective VH-11/8, regarding production, and procurement of resources for said production, of Phyx©. Initial launch campaigns for Terrestrial Markets to target Metropols 10 through F-700.

Proceed with following directives effective immediately:

A: Increased pressure on internal employees at Civic Security Companies – All Xiotron©®™SM payroll recipients that currently hold positions at Security Companies, including, but not limited to: Velor & Gaston®, Global Defense Corporation®, ÆrrowSoft™, Beckler & Josch™, etc. to minimize property threat and damage by militants operating in Metropols.

B: Increase security for CryoCom® facilities, personnel, and equipment; to and from loading zones, including but not limited to: Space Ports, Processing Facilities, Cargo Exchange Locations, etc.

C: Secure funding for larger processing plant in the Mare Imbrium / Apennine Mountain Region, Zone 003-7.

D: Secure legality through Corporate Lobbying in Corporate-controlled government sectors for - Processing of Hominid Bio-Material for Medicinal Usage.

E: Ensure universal censorship of contradicting research on health concerns for Phyx© product.

Subsection A – Issue 1 [Concerning Viizor™ & Asc.] Dictation for A1 Metropol Sector Heads:

A: Regarding the targeting of High Population Areas (HPAs) with Phyx©, to produce population-wide dependency, securing sales for duration of population's life-span.

B: Allow/encourage overpopulation of 'A' Historic Districts.

C: Implement strict pro-health security measures to combat statistical increase of infectious diseases.

D: Hire Xiotron©®™SM approved Individual Contractors to locate and procure qualifying units of population to be processed at secured facilities. {Xiotron©®™SM reserves the Corporate Right [CRB-55/3k], to retain information from: The

Government, & Corporate Entities, et al, both terrestrial, alien, or undiscovered sentient lifeform of legal understanding, as well as individuals of the population of this, or any celestial body - to ensure the safety, and anonymity, of clients and staff.}

E: Media black-out regarding patients–" "Alright, Automota, that's enough." Good christ. I glanced over at my guest. "So, what, the big corps that own the world, are planning to get people addicted to a drug that is actually made from the bodies of those same people? And they are going to use the toxic whirlpool of drug addiction, promiscuity, cramped living spaces, and poverty to foster unhealthy population growth; probably fake a plague or something, use the heightened security as leeway to send in the jump-out-boys to bag "targeted" citizens, and turn them into drugs to help soothe the terrified populace? Oh, and they process their evil drug, made from people, at their moon-base.

Am I getting that right? Cause chaos, profit from said chaos?" She leaned her head back in the seat, seemingly enjoying the ride. Thin wisps of velvety smoke drifted from her barely parted lips; drifting away into the ever-rushing wind. "Yeah, Johnny, that's why we hate you; because *you're* the *jump-out-boys*." Still leaning back, she rolled her head to face me, kissed the air, and winked.

"We have to take out Curden." Laughter rang out from the small woman, "You're fucking kidding, right? Milton Curden, *the* corrupt cop to trump all corrupt cops? You want to, what, storm Precinct 21? Ha! With who?" She looked around. "Hey! We could stuff that loader with explosives, and drive it straight through the front doors '*BOOM!*' Their whole day, ruined. But that probably wouldn't get Curden, he's probably on too high of a floor. Or maybe-" "Are you some kind of lunatic? Chill the fuck out, we aren't going all bonkers and blowing up the city and people to *'save the city and people.'* I swear, you reactionaries are some fuckin' heroes, huh? Literally, retarded." She looked at me in a funny way, "You know, you should join the Underground, we could use a guy like you." For a moment, I had to think about it. In all fairness, I was already about to be ostracized from the whole of society as a criminal, so what was the big deal with going a step further and joining some terror-cell? It's not every day that a guy gets offered to join an anti-establishment renegade force. Who knows, they may even give me a promotion.

We pulled up to the service entrance of the Hospital in 20B, followed by Tracy in the loader. A few orderlies were hanging around like bums, having a smoke. I called out from the car, "Hey, there's emergency patients requiring Cryo-Med in the bed of the loader. Get to it, ASAP." "And y–" Before the tubby bastard could spout off, I held my badge up.

"GDC, stop fucking around." "Y-yessir!" They scrambled to figure out what to do. Not my problem. Tracy was unloading her weapons from the cab, taking her sweet time. "Come on, *sweetheart*, we've got shit to do." Strutting over to the open-top convertible, "I should pepper your shit with lead. Oh, hey, hun, how was the nap?" A puzzled expression came across my prisoner's face. I turned my head to the ditsy Android, "Tracy-" "It's fucking *Trish!*" "Whatever, get in the back and make it a machine-gun nest." We pealed out of the hospital, ushered by the roar of that magnificent engine.

I needed to come up with a plan, so let's see who's available to die tonight: Myself, Tracy, Automota, and... "Hey, *outlaw*, I never got your name." Her smudged red lips glistening in the flashing of passing city-lights let out the name, "Aphid." Cut-off by that talking trashcan, "Hiya, I'm Trish, nice to meet you!" Robotically, she craned herself in between the front seats, offering her hand to Aphid. "H-holy shit, you're an Android!" The woman seemed terrified, pushing herself up against the cardoor, trying desperately to put as much space between herself and Tracy as possible. You can never really tell if it's a 'droid or not, until you see the eyes. "Th-those are programmed to kill, aren't they?! Why is it here?!" "At-ease, little soldier, it's not a military model." Exhaling, I went back to focusing on the road as the girls got acquainted. "Yeah, I was programmed for, uh, entertainment." Tracy returned to her reclined seating-position in the back. Slightly relaxing, Aphid glanced back at Tracy. "You don't behave like the average pleasure model, Trish." "See, Johnny, she's known me for all of ten minutes, and *she* remembers my fucking name. Ass-hat. Anyway, this *'knight of moral duty'* over here," Tracy motioned at me as Aphid stretched her neck to peer into the back seat, "was kind enough to unlock my learning capacity, or some such thing. I'm sort of

obligated to help him, but he's like a friend, I guess."
"Get bent, Tracy." I exhaled. After a long discussion on my idea, we had finally hashed out a rough plan. But hey, no plan survives its first encounter with the enemy.

Zooming along the highway, I zoned out, one last daydream, one last time to pretend like I'm gonna make it big. I've stated before that time was just a highway, and I was taking a detour. I think my detour goes a bit offroad. Drowning out the sound of the chattering females, I turned the sound on the RadCom™ up. I wanted to hear her song one more time before my life changed forever. The headlights rushed along the black, serpentine roadways, slicing through the thick darkness of the polluted city night. Over the next urban horizon, I could see the GDC tower, gleaming like a beacon in the night. "Ready, ladies?"

"Yep!" "*Ooh, yeah.*" "Yeah."

Chapter 16

Pulling into an alley about a block away, I parked Automota, but left her engine on. Hopping out, I adjusted my jacket and went around to the trunk. -*pop*- "Let's see, what fits in the coat... the SBR, the side-by-side sawed-off shotty, aaand, another pistol... ooh, and some of this..." I loaded up. "Now, don't wreck my car, Tracy." "Ooo, *nobody's wreckin' me. See ya soon, sugar, kiss-kiss.*" Tracy blew a kiss too, as they took off down the alley and around a corner. I hope that wasn't going to be the last time I saw that car.

I went to reach for my smokes, fuck. I had left the fresh pack in the cup holder. I guess I was smoking the second-to-last in that 'emergency pack.' -*flick*- Taking a long, hard drag, I started my walk toward the precinct. Hands in my pockets, cig in my mouth, heh, almost reminds me of going to work. It was one of those nights where the wind was just nippy enough to make you tense up. Rain was in the air preceded currently by a typical mist hanging in the city streets and alleys. The street-lamps flickered, some were never on. Passing trashcans and urchins alike, I hastened my pace. Emerging onto the main street, I was faced by the monolith; Precinct 21. Hiking up the front stairs, I couldn't help but liken myself to a hero assaulting the Ivory Tower of some evil wizard. Wu-chin always called me a hero; guess he was right, crazy old bastard. I flicked the spent butt to the side as I entered the automatic doors.

"Special Jurisdictions Unit 88, Agent, Peiler, Johnathan; what a pleasure to see you tonight. Is there anything I can prepare for you while you are en route to your destination?" "Nothing tonight, Penny, I'm here to see Curden. It's urgent, and no, there is no scheduled appointment." *"Understood, agent. Please see yourself to the elevator, and enjoy your stay."* A brisk air hit my face as the elevator opened; here we go.

It seemed like the longest elevator ride I've ever had. An eternity, it seemed, that I was ascending this building. What if the plan fucks up? What if they spring it early? It doesn't matter, it's all or nothing now.

'You have arrived at the
Eighty-third
floor. Please exist with care!'

Stepping off the lift, I stopped for a moment to admire the view again. An endless sea of neon spires, pulsating with veins of light, spreading across the city. The fact that Curden had smooth jazz playing in the office made the moment all the more surreal. Hearing the elevator doors shut behind me I immediately spun about, and from my pockets produced two small cakes of C4 with a little remote trigger contraption. Placing both on the lift-doors, I turned and walked speedily for Milton's seating area. A fearsome heat and deafening blast rocked the building, sending shards of glass and metal shrapnel into the night sky. Clicking the trigger was satisfying, but I had a short time to act at this point; the security teams would swarm this place in no-time flat. Crashing and clanging could be heard bellowing from the elevator shaft, as the lift tumbled eighty-some floors down. Smoke poured from the shattered glass-wall that was infront of the elevator; the plumes were probably visible to half the district. Alarms of all kinds started sounding. Running into the conference area, "Hey, Curden, you fucking prick, where are ya?" His egg-chair whirled around, revealing a shocked Milton staring at me with blood-shot jaundiced eyes. Mouth gaping open, "What in the fuck is going on here, Johnny, what the fuck did you do to my office?!" "You could use some remodeling, Milt. Before I fucking kill you — you know, for that whole child-trafficking thing, and big corp conspiracy to harm the general public more than it already does — I just want to know, *why*. Why, Milt? What made you do it?" He started to chuckle, "So, you found out about the Protocols, huh? Haha, well, you gotta admit, J Man, it's a crafty plan. Crafty indeed, and it'll guarantee big profits..." "You want me to enslave humanity for some money? What do you take me for?" "Well, Johnny, up until this point, I took you for a decently smart man. But, here, turns out that you're nothin' but a punk bitch with a hero-complex. You're already 'enslaved,' you fucking hamster! You don't see the walls around you? Every fucking housing complex, every ad-billboard, all the ways people are enslaved through entertainment? No? You have come so far as to kill me because I was abducting the tainted offspring of *fucking prostitutes* – doing the place a *favour*, might I add — but you never even saw the bigger picture? Even 97, yes, another son-of-a-whore that, through my good fucking graces, found solace in his usefulness to the eternal machine that we all serve. Everything that happens has been planned out, you don't get it. God is real, John, very real. And what he is, is a collective conscious that rules the world; and that collective conscious can be accessed through one's particular ability to exploit the given system. And, eventually, get hired on with Xiotron©®™℠... The guards are coming J-Money, and you won't have any place to run!" he hissed from his chair, teeth gritting as he seethed. Reaching into my coat, I pulled out the shotgun, and loosely aimed it in my boss's direction.

Surprisingly, Curden stood up, to his full, lanky figure. A practical Scarecrow, he was well over two metres, but spindly as spiders legs. He crept towards me. "Listen, Johnathan, you need to understand the revelation that is this Plan. It solves the over-population problem by recycling the population into itself. You see, by taking excess young from the herd, and utilizing it to produce a sedative for the herd itself, it becomes cyclical. We can control the population entirely this way. It'll be a stagnant, controllable population, with predictable GDP and market sectors. Think of the controlled-growth possibilities, it's a miracle, an act of God, John, the wisdom of a divine guidance." My hands tensed up on the weapon. "Do you fucking hear yourself right now? You're talking of killing people to help better enslave other people, for GDP! And why?" Holding the gun a little higher, "Why kids? Why kids, Milt?! Why are they all kids?!" Putting his hands up to indicate he was empty-handed, "Beats me, Johnny, you fuckin' moron. I'm not an expert in chemical biology. How the fuck should I know why they harvest kids specifically? Does it look like I'm in charge or something?" It had slipped my mind; that Milton wasn't very high on the corporate ladder.

Curden wasn't a mastermind, or some big-shot; he was a money-hungry junkie; human garbage, preying on the weak. Angrily, I charged towards him. Curden fled, backing himself up against the window-wall. "Now listen Johnny! What is it, huh? You want more money? Wha-" "It isn't about money, you spineless thrall! You're a corrupt fucking bastard. And guess what, the whole *fucking* world is going to see that document, and Viizor™'s stocks will tank. You'll be destitute. Even if I don't kill you, you'll be ruined." "And you, Johnny, you'll be out of a job, haha." Sprawling himself out against the glass, Curden chuckled to himself, as if there wasn't a gun a metre from his face. "The joke is on you, Curden; if I live through this bullshit, I invested two hundred thousand in BioDyme®, and when Viizor™ tanks from complications regarding child trafficking, guess whose stocks jump? That's right – hedge your bets, Milt." Any semblance of a smirk that was on his face, vanished. His face was drooping with disdain.

Grinding his already-eroded teeth together, Curden sleazed, "You've probably got to be the most self-centred, dumb, shortsighted, narrowminded, uh... fuck... uhh... infidel! Yes! An Infidel, Heretic, Defiler! You are against the Gods of your Time Johnny! Haha! And God is on my side! ***My** fucking* side! And soon..." A slimy, eel-like purple tongue, lubricated his lips for another round of ravings, "...and soon, haha, soon, Johnny, God's many gun-toting angels, will be upon thee. And unfortunately for you, '*o sinner,*' the Wrath of God is extra-judicial." He was right; I didn't have much time to get the info I wanted, so I'd have to cut the theatrics. "What happened to Amasaka and van Dreer? And stop fucking with me Milton!" Shoving the gun in his direction, I cocked the hammers back. The corporate ghoul, pressed himself harder against the glass. "Your petty threats are nothing to me; the *Hand of God* in this city! I practically run GDC, J-sack; do you get that?" Raising the gun a bit, "I'm about to cut off God's hand for stealing from me and the people! Now, tell me what happened to those agents, Mr. Investigative Head P21!" Ever so slightly, he started to chuckle, laugh, and wheeze, "Haha, heh, well, I killed them. All of them." I had to hold back the desire to dump two rounds into his chest; I still needed answers. "How long, then, how many agents?" "Hehe, this has been goin' on a long time Johnny, for a long time. I've had to liquidate many assets. People start asking questions, get nosy, some get violent... I knew I could never buy you, not truly. So I coerced you into doing my bidding. I thought for a second you had become a changed man after you got a taste of some money. But, I knew, in the back of my fucking mind, you were always the 'good cop,' never going to back down from a fight against injustice, perceived or otherwise. And look, look at how right I am! I took you on, and now, not long after, you've popped explosives off in my office and have me at gunpoint, threatening to take down the entire operation! Well, too bad you won't live to finish the job!" Darting from side to side, Curden's eyes were going wild; he needed a Phyx©. Milton's eyes stopped jumping for a moment and locked with mine. "Your first partner, she was the first one to build the case on the missing kids; you know that, it's why you give a shit. Haha, she had to go, Johnny, she knew too much." A maniacal grin spread across his face; he knew he had struck a nerve. I was working for her killer this entire time, and I never even knew it. Volcanic rage boiled within me. Inching towards the office-goon, he crept backwards along the glass away from the barrel of my gun. "You took her from me... You took her from me! I'll kill you Milton, you sniveling parasite! You don't deserve to live after all the lives you've stolen! You deceiver, lying, piece-a' shit!"

Sliding along the glass-wall, Milton was cast against a brilliant view of the city-scape. If I wasn't in a hefty rage, I'd probably stop to appreciate the picturesque view before me. Laughter whistled through his splintered teeth. "It's over, John, you can kill me, but you can't stop the big corps. It's bigger than us Johnny, you're insignificant. Hehehah!" I couldn't hold back. All of my pent up aggression, frustration, hate, all of it; let loose. Dropping my shotgun, I bull-rushed Curden. I didn't care if the guards were coming to kill me, I didn't care if I was late for the rendezvous – I needed revenge. I fell on him like water from a broken dam. The sound of his body taking blow after blow was magnified in the minimalist setting. Against the backdrop of sirens, only the screaming of a man in dire straits and excruciating pain could be heard. Every terrible thing I hated about this world, I saw on his face. The glass-wall began to crack as Milton's head banged up against it repeatedly following each unrestrained blow from my fist. Moments later, I had probably broken his jaw, most of his teeth, and who knows what else. I kept swinging. After a bit of that, I pulled his beaten frame to its feet, and braced him against the glass. Blood poured from his mouth, leaking crimson from every gaping facial wound, smearing it; the colour popping out against the white floor. A couple of tooth-fragments fell to the ground, making little clicks as they hit. His uniform was torn, stained and soaked with that liquid of life. I picked up the gun and took aim. Curden was leaning against the glass, knees bent, hands like a lizard, trying to keep himself up. His head hung low, eyes puffy from bruising. He was flushed, practically exsanguinated. Labouring to lift his own head, he spat out another tooth, and some blood. Wiping his mouth on his sleeve, he wheezed a strained chuckle, "It doesn't matter any more, heheh." Spitting again, he grinned, "I've seen the plan, I know what's coming. I know how things play out from here. Bullets won't work, John; you cannot kill it with weapons. I have seen the effects of Phyx© on the populace, haha, and myself. I no longer require eyes to see, John. I have been shown Paradise. I know what Eden was..." Twitching, and lurching his head about; his jaw cracking,

"Heaven is devoid of light, John."

My finger ran over both triggers.

Millions of shards of glass accompanied Curden's body as it was defenestrated violently. The blast took out roughly a three-metre-wide section of the window. Walking to the edge, I peered over just in-time to see Milton's body explode on impact all over those marble steps down below. At that moment, a massive quake rocked the building and the lights went out. Stumbling forward I braced myself against the opening in the glass-wall; the shotgun tumbled from my bloody hands, disappearing over the edge. "Ha, guess they pulled it off." Rain drops caressed my tired face, as I breathed in the wind above the city. With the power out, you could really admire the surrounding lights and buildings. In retrospect, I probably should have told Curden, right before I blew him away, I had instructed upon my death that my shares in

BioDyme® go to the only guy that always greeted me with a smile: old man Wu-chin. Such an act of generosity would have driven him to kill himself. I knew that taking down the system was someone else's job, but at least I sent a message to their corrupt cronies. The neon from the advertisements, signs, and buildings, lit up my shades as I peered out over the open city skyline. Sounds of boots filing into formation behind me overpowered the screaming of still-wailing sirens. "Agent Peiler! You are under arrest for the murder of Investigative Head, Milton Curden; and the orchestration of a terrorist attack on the corporate assets of the Global Defense Corporation®. We are authorized to ensure your compliance."

"You know, boys, you've really got it all wrong, and one day, hopefully, you'll realize that." Looking down at myself, I noticed that a bunch of little, red laser-dots were peppering me. "You aren't authorized to speak, Agent." "I'm not authorized to do a lot of things, *officer*." Staring down to the glistening, rain-soaked city below; I had to think if I could have done it differently. It doesn't matter now, heh, probably never did. Wish I could have sat in my chair, one last time. One last drive in Automota. There's a lot of things I wish, right now. Could be worse, you know? At least I'm not in a gutter. Reaching into my coat, I pulled out the beaten-up cigarette box. My thumb wiped the rain droplets from the cellophane coating on the box - *Outer Rim*™ - *Taste the Galaxy* © - Too bad I never got to taste it. Putting one to my lips, I went to light it. "Don't move, Agent!" My cigarette bobbed up and down as I retorted, "I'll do whatever the fuck I want..." Bringing the lighter closer to the end of the cig, I could hear the racking of bolts, and the switching-off of safeties; the Machine-gun Orchestra was ready to play me out." "Agent! Don't move...!" I had to chuckle; last smoke after all...

    -flick-

Exist with care!